Orgy at the STD Clinic

Todd Tillotson is struggling to move on after his husband is killed in a hit and run attack a year earlier during a Black Lives Matter protest in Seattle.

In this novel set entirely on public transportation, we watch as Todd, isolated throughout the pandemic, battles desperation in his attempt to safely reconnect with the world.

Will he find love again, even casual friendship, or will he simply end up another crazy old man on the bus?

Things don't look good until a man whose face he can't even see sits down beside him despite the raging variants.

And asks him a question that will change his life.

Praise for Johnny Townsend

In *Zombies for Jesus*, "Townsend isn't writing satire, but deeply emotional and revealing portraits of people who are, with a few exceptions, quite lovable."

Kel Munger, *Sacramento News and Review*

In *Sex among the Saints,* "Townsend writes with a deadpan wit and a supple, realistic prose that's full of psychological empathy….he takes his protagonists' moral struggles seriously and invests them with real emotional resonance."

Kirkus Reviews

Let the Faggots Burn: The UpStairs Lounge Fire is "a gripping account of all the horrors that transpired that night, as well as a respectful remembrance of the victims."

Terry Firma, *Patheos*

"Johnny Townsend's 'Partying with St. Roch' [in the anthology *Latter-Gay Saints*] tells a beautiful, haunting tale."

Kent Brintnall, *Out in Print: Queer Book Reviews*

Selling the City of Enoch is "sharply intelligent…pleasingly complex…The stories are full of…doubters, but there's no vindictiveness in these pages; the characters continuously poke holes in Mormonism's more extravagant absurdities, but they take very little pleasure in doing so….Many of Townsend's stories…have a provocative edge to them, but this [book] displays a great deal of insight as well…a playful, biting and surprisingly warm collection."

Kirkus Reviews

Gayrabian Nights is "an allegorical tour de force…a hard-core emotional punch."

Gay. Guy. Reading and Friends

The Washing of Brains has "A lovely writing style, and each story [is] full of unique, engaging characters….immensely entertaining."

Rainbow Awards

In *Dead Mankind Walking*, "Townsend writes in an energetic prose that balances crankiness and humor….A rambunctious volume of short, well-crafted essays…"

Kirkus Reviews

Orgy at the STD Clinic

Johnny Townsend

Trenton, Georgia

Print ISBN: 978-1-64719-938-8
Ebook ISBN: 978-1-64719-939-5

Published by BookLocker.com, Inc., Trenton, Georgia, U.S.A.

Printed on acid-free paper.

BookLocker.com, Inc.

2022

First Edition

Cover art and design by Laceoni

To Bob,

the first bus driver

to fuck me

Special thanks to Robert Ramsay,
Donna Banta, and Jeff Laver
for their editorial assistance

For more of Robert's work,
please read *Wreck of the Royal Express.*

For more of Donna's work,
please read *Seer Stone.*

For more of Jeff's work,
please read *A Happier Year.*

Contents

Chapter One: The Road to Hell

"If you're going to drive me to suicide," I said, "the least you could do is provide the pills."

The man, about forty, strong and with worrisome muscles stretching through his Sonics T-shirt, stared at me. He was medium brown to my pale tan and, since he wasn't wearing a mask, I could see his jaw drop in surprise.

Then the corners of his mouth turned up slightly.

"I'm going to give you a pass," he said, "because you're crazy."

He continued two rows past me down the aisle and plopped onto a seat on the left side of the bus. "Mother*fucker*," he muttered, but with a lighthearted tone, and I heard a woman near him laugh.

Odd that one could hear a black accent even in a laugh.

A white man across the aisle from me sneezed. No accent in the sneeze that I could detect. I wondered if non-white folks could tell.

A Latino sitting behind me banged on the window and shouted through the glass at someone on the street he recognized.

Like everyone else, I hated riding the bus. But I hated driving even more, so I'd sold my last car twenty years earlier. I could pay a lot of cab fare, I'd thought at the time, with the money I saved not paying car insurance.

Only I never hired a cab. Or an Uber or a Lyft. Or a Logger, the comparable system popular here in Seattle.

The bus swerved to avoid a pothole.

Ding!

I saw the Stop Requested sign light up, and a tiny Asian woman, old, crept to the rear exit one row ahead of me, hanging on carefully with every step.

A side exit, really, despite the name.

Back in Italy, the rear exit had truly been at the rear of the bus.

As the driver approached the stop without slowing, the woman's head swiveled about in confusion. She raised her free hand a few inches and then dropped it as if reprimanded.

"This is my stop!" I called out.

The driver slowed quickly, the woman bumping against the plexiglass next to the exit but maintaining her balance. The driver's eyes scanned the bus in her rearview mirror. "Sorry," she said.

When the doors opened, the elderly Asian woman hopped down onto the sidewalk and shuffled away.

"No problem," I called back.

The driver waited a second longer. I knew she was expecting me to leave, too, the voice she'd heard clearly not that of an elderly Asian woman, but I was too tired to explain. The driver either figured it out or gave up because she finally closed the doors and drove on.

"Hey."

I turned to look behind me. The black man who'd threatened to kill me a few moments earlier after I'd asked him to wear a mask now offered his fist. He nodded an apology.

I touched my fist to his, returning the nod. Then he sat back down, and I looked out the window again.

We passed an apartment building under construction, and a convenience store, and a smoke shop.

Two police officers were talking to a black man in front of a taco truck.

I closed my eyes.

No one was waiting for me at home.

***

I was halfway to the corner before I realized I'd left my bus pass on the coffee table.

Mannaggia.

I quickly jogged back, grabbed the purple lanyard holding my work badge and Orca card, and started back for the bus stop. Ever since Brigham and I had moved into our house in Rainier Beach fifteen years earlier, I'd been able to cut across the front yard of the Lutheran church on the corner. It saved both time and, more importantly, fifty yards of uphill effort to reach the sharply angled corner.

Walking was generally an easy, low-stress exercise, but because I carried so much extra weight in my belly, the strain on my knees was enormous. I'd heard that large-breasted women often experienced chronic back pain because their extra weight was all up front. But even 40DD breasts only weighed three to four pounds each. I carried the equivalent of twenty-three Dolly Parton breasts well forward of my natural center of gravity. Without a counterbalancing tail sufficient to stabilize an Ornithomimus, my back was aching long before I could burn enough calories to make a difference.

The church on the corner had been sold to a "troubled youth" organization a few years before the pandemic. Then the economic upheaval of worldwide disease forced the youth organization to sell to an Orthodox Ethiopian congregation. And those dedicated folks were at church almost every day. At the crack of dawn.

Even if the worshippers were inside when I cut across the property, it still felt inappropriate.

So I trudged up the hill.

The 106 thundered past on Renton Avenue.

"Dannazione!"

In public, I tried to curse in Italian so as not to offend anyone within earshot. But my Mormon missionary training didn't offer much to work with. "Pick!" and "Flip!" weren't even Italian.

Fortunately, I'd found the book *Merde!* years ago at Half Price Books. It provided the necessary instruction that had been lacking at the Missionary Training Center.

On our first anniversary, I'd pieced together a quilt for Brigham in the shape of a sign: "Missionary Position Training Center." We liked having sex on top of it. Sometimes in our old temple garments.

I almost didn't go out with Brigham after learning his first name.

He almost didn't go out with me when I told him I was ex-Mormon, too.

Then, after we discovered we'd both served in the Italy Rome Mission, we agreed to try a first date.

No longer in a rush to catch the 7:31, I strolled the rest of the way to the bus stop. I could hear deep, male voices humming inside the church. Lots of basses in there.

I missed my days in the Seattle Men's Chorus. I'd stopped participating when I gave up my car, even though Brigham offered to drive me.

Above and beyond the church parking lot, I could barely make out Mt. Baker in the distance, covered in snow and visible only a few times a year. Of course, a clear sky brought its own problems. I stepped off the curb and inched into the street to position myself in the shadow of the bus stop sign, trying to shield my face from the already hot morning sun.

108 degrees last week in Seattle. But at least it wasn't the 121 they'd suffered up in British Columbia. My friend Jeremy in Surrey talked often of moving to the countryside and had even looked at property in Lytton. Thank God he wasn't there when most of the town was destroyed.

It felt some days as if the whole world was heading toward the Bridge of San Luis Rey.

At 7:46, another 106 pulled up. The muscular Asian driver had a buzz cut and wore a shirt heavily starched with testosterone. Self-assurance could be sexy regardless of body type, but I was no longer able to muster any, and the driver didn't look twice at me.

Gaydar didn't work unless a few pings could hit their target. It was like looking into a cave without a light source. Anything could be in there.

Anything but interest.

Boo hoo.

Always something, as Gilda used to say.

An old black woman with a grocery cart sat in the disabled section, dutifully wearing her mask. The next several seats were occupied mostly by young Asians, all glued to their cell phones, most of them also masking.

A middle-aged white woman with her mask below her nose sat in the last row before the rear exit. She was one of the regulars and always sat with one leg blocking half the aisle, glaring challenges at everyone who boarded. No one would have sat next to her even if the empty seat beside her was the only one available.

I passed the insolent leg and climbed up a step to sit in the row directly beyond the door, one of my favorite spots. The wall of the bus here partially shielded me from the sun.

I'd hardly had the chance to set my bag down when the driver pulled over to the next stop. I watched as Tommy climbed aboard and cursed myself for missing the earlier bus, casually turning my work badge around to make sure no one could read it. Tommy's eyes lit up when he saw me, and he hurried down the aisle, swinging onto the seat beside me.

He kissed me—mask to mask—and squeezed my thigh.

"How are you today?" I asked.

"Horny," he said. Loudly, as usual. I wasn't sure if Tommy had Tourette's or Asperger's or both. He was white, around forty, with mutton chops and scruffy brown hair. He'd first kissed me on the sidewalk up on Capitol Hill when he was twenty-five. I'd never been a fan of cringe comedy, and Tommy offered little other than cringe drama, which was far less appealing.

"I'm sorry to hear that." I tried not to overemphasize the word "hear." Perhaps this would be the end of the conversation.

"My boss yelled at me yesterday."

I didn't want to ask.

I didn't ask.

Tommy leaned into me and rested his head on my shoulder. I reached over and held his hand until we pulled up to his stop.

***

Ah, I liked this driver. A white guy, maybe fifty, with a shaved head and a longish white beard. By itself, that might not have been enough, but he always wore a tight shirt, the buttons threatening to rip right out. Through the little diamond-shaped windows formed by the battle between fabric and buttons, I could see a muscular if thin chest, and hints of a beautiful hair pattern.

I no longer wore shirts with buttons.

"Morning," I said, leaning down to tap my Orca card.

The driver didn't respond.

In my younger days, I could cruise men in passing cars while waiting for the bus. Helped a lot of guys get their days off to a good start. It was how I'd first met Brigham, after all. Now I was invisible, even when people had to deal with me directly.

Not the same as it was for Ralph Ellison, but I understood his title a bit more now. It worked so much better than *Totally Unimportant and Valueless Man*, which was perhaps more accurate but less literary.

On the corner of 51st, an Asian man carrying two garbage bags full of clothes boarded. He was also juggling a small bottle of laundry detergent and a book he was probably planning on reading during the two-hour ordeal ahead of him. *Interior Chinatown.*

I wondered if laundromats were a good place to pick up guys.

On Rainier, the driver let on two more passengers but then closed the door in someone else's face. I could hear shouting from the sidewalk.

"Put on your mask!" the driver shouted back.

The man pounded on the door while the driver waited. After another moment of pounding, followed by a moment of calm, the driver opened the door, and a black man in his fifties boarded. His shirt was wrinkled, and he walked with a wide stance, as if a long, invisible board were attached to his ankles, forcing them apart.

He slammed the plexiglass door protecting the driver, defiantly pulled off his cloth mask, and then grabbed a handful of paper masks from the dispenser and threw them into the air like confetti. They floated down onto other passengers, several seats, and the floor.

The guy stomped down the aisle, his feet still separated by the invisible board.

The driver waited for him to sit down and then pulled away from the curb.

I wished I was the kind of person the driver would have sought comfort from at the end of his shift.

I'd need to exit through the rear at my stop, but perhaps I could hurry up to the front again before he closed the door to new riders and hand him a slip of paper with my name and number. Maybe he did need comforting but was too professional to let on. If he had my number, he *might* call.

He certainly wouldn't if he didn't have it.

I tried to work up my nerve over the next twenty minutes. Then, when I pulled the cord for my stop, the glucose sensor attached to my upper left arm popped off and hit the window.

Porca la miseria. I'd just attached the 14-day sensor that morning. Newly activated sensors took an hour to calibrate. I hadn't even gotten one reading off the damn thing. And my insurance didn't cover the cost. I paid out of pocket because I hated pricking my fingers three times a day.

I tossed the ruined sensor into my bag, stepped off the bus, and headed for Bay 2.

***

When the bus pulled up to the curb and opened its doors, I paused just a moment to make sure no one needed to exit out the front. When the pandemic began, riders were ordered to exit only out the rear, and most drivers kept their plexiglass shield extended to block folks from coming out the front. But some riders, even those with no apparent disability, still insisted on exiting through the front.

If the sun was hitting the windows at a certain angle, it was difficult from the sidewalk to see what was happening inside, but since I didn't notice any motion in the forward part of the bus, I started walking toward the front steps.

Beep, beep, beep, beep.

The driver was lowering the front of the bus. Apparently, there *was* a disabled person coming out. I waited patiently but still detected no movement. Then I saw the driver waving me aboard.

The driver had lowered the bus for *me*. And now I could see it was the Native American driver who was rude on almost every occasion. Once, when I unsuccessfully tapped my Orca card three times without getting an approval, he yelled at me. "Put some money on your damn card!"

"I have a monthly pass," I told him.

"Then tap your card right!"

Another time, I'd boarded carrying a single bag of groceries along with a case of lemon seltzer water. Two seconds after I tapped my card, the driver slammed the doors shut and threw his foot against the accelerator. I'd dropped the case of seltzer water trying to keep myself from falling. Two cans started fizzing all across the aisle.

"Stupid!" the driver had yelled.

So I knew exactly why he'd lowered the front of the bus today. Seattleites were nothing if not passive aggressive.

I climbed up the steps, tapped my card, and nodded politely to the driver. "Bitch," I said.

He slapped the plexiglass door protecting him from the riff raff. "You want a piece of me?"

He thought he was George Costanza's father.

"Thanks for offering," I said. "I'm partial to cocks. But I'll take a piece of your ass if you'd rather." I held out my hand. "Wanna give me your number?"

And I judged Tommy for behaving poorly in public.

The driver faced forward again and jammed his foot on the accelerator. I was prepared, of course, but I still made an exaggerated pretense at catching myself. "Trying to get my legs in the air already?" I asked. "We should probably do this when you're not working."

I made my way to a free seat midway into the bus. I'd been an asshole, I realized, and I was absolutely fine with it.

Chapter Two: The Road to Ruin

The Latina passenger across the aisle from me lowered her gaze and stared. Without the ability to see her entire face, I wasn't sure exactly what emotion she was conveying, but it wasn't elation.

She wasn't looking at "me," though, at least not my face, so I looked down to determine what she *was* looking at.

I was picking at a scab on my left forearm, and it was bleeding ever so slightly.

Mortified, I stopped and turned to look out the window. In the months after Brigham's murder, I'd slowly developed an excoriation disorder. I picked for no apparent reason, the same way some folks chewed their nails or pulled out strands of hair.

In my case, of course, it led to bleeding and scarring, both off-putting. I'd seen a counselor twice, but it was so hard to travel to appointments that I found myself delaying the next one.

I pulled out my phone and sent myself a note to call the clinic on my lunch break. My glasses fogged easily during the commute, so I tried not to text much while on the bus. Too many typos.

Or, worse, autocorrect. I hadn't meant to ask Jeremy to send me a picture of his tree. He liked *trains*, could wait for hours at a trestle for just the right shot, and I appreciated his dedication.

Autocorrect always seemed especially capricious, perhaps the first example of sentient AI. I hadn't meant to text Brigham, "Seed you tonight," when we set up our first official date.

But it had worked out OK.

I hit Send and turned to look back out the window. Flowers and candles surrounded a light pole next to a bus stop. Someone, it seemed, had been killed there in the last day or two.

***

A maskless passenger advanced as I retreated, wielding her, "I have an immune system!" like a weapon. The woman was probably in her late forties, thirty pounds overweight, and believed in coloring her hair a shade of blonde that would not have looked natural even if she were twenty.

All I'd done was point to the mask dispenser beside the train doors when she coughed on a commuter who was exiting at the same time she was boarding.

Don't kick against the pricks, I remembered reading decades ago. I'd taught the Elders' Quorum for over a year after returning from my mission.

"Drug companies are just trying to make money!" the woman shouted. I could feel a drop of spittle hitting my arm. I hoped no pathogens entered through one of my self-inflicted wounds.

"Are you talking about capitalism?" I asked. Here at the headquarters of Starbucks and Boeing and Microsoft and Costco. I had such trouble following the logic of some arguments. Those on the right were supposed to *like* the motivation of profit.

I closed my eyes.

Why in the world was I engaging with this crazy person? There was no Brigham to join in Paradise, or Spirit Prison, or anywhere. And I didn't *really* want to leave, did I? Or I wouldn't be wearing a mask, either.

"Like Amazon?" I asked.

The woman screamed as if her body were being physically ripped apart. Several passengers retreated into the next car, but others were trapped behind me at the end of this one.

"Hospitals get a bonus when someone gets COVID!" the woman shouted. "And then they mine hormones from them!"

I remembered as a teen reading one of Robert A. Heinlein's last novels, *The Number of the Beast*, in which I first learned the concept of alternative universes.

How had we ended up in one where insanity was the norm?

My heart pounding, I considered suggesting the woman start advocating for universal healthcare. Once a missionary, always a missionary. Instead, I nodded slowly, with broad movements. The woman hesitated just a second, not quite ready to stop arguing but apparently unsure if she'd already won or not. I'd say it was easy to confuse delusional people, but in truth, it was easy to confuse just about anyone.

I'd believed Richard when he told me he'd caught gonorrhea from absentmindedly gnawing on his coworker's ink pen. That was long before I met Brigham. Richard also brought crabs home one day after switching chairs with his coworker.

I tried to keep my voice casual. "You're absolutely right," I said.

The woman frowned, her lips twitching.

Not as charming as Samantha Stevens's nose.

Before she could recover, I added, just as casually, though my chest hurt now, "You know who else has immune systems?" I didn't allow even a rhetorical pause and pushed on. "The million or so people who die of tetanus every year." I was about to try squeezing in some numbers about measles and diphtheria but never got the chance.

The woman lunged at me and ripped off my mask, spitting in my face.

Had I read somewhere once that misery was a more reliable source of mental illness than genetics?

When her fingernails drew blood, I grabbed the woman's hands and said, so low she quieted down to listen. "I sure hope you don't catch my HIV."

***

Earbud day.

Pink singing "Just Give Me a Reason" and "What About Us?"

Kelly Clarkson singing "Walk Away" and "Since U Been Gone."

OneRepublic singing, "Love Runs Out."

But even listening to Sara Bareilles singing "Brave" couldn't erase the horror of seeing yet another name added to the yard full of signs I passed every day insisting we "Say Her Name."

***

I gasped when a light-skinned Indian boarded the bus along MLK. In the second before he pulled his mask up, I thought I was looking at Ramesh again.

Ramesh wasn't really my friend. And we'd never had sex, though he was stunningly beautiful and I'd sure fantasized about it. He was part of the package deal when I started dating Brigham. They'd known one another for almost ten years already by that point. He and Brigham continued to see each other for dinner once every month or so. I joined a couple of times a year.

But when Brigham was attacked during a Black Lives Matter protest up on Capitol Hill, I inherited Ramesh.

He inherited me, too.

For a while, we tried developing our friendship in an effort to keep the memory of Brigham alive. Only we didn't particularly like each other. If we had, we wouldn't have waited so long to begin with.

Still, I became part of the "Squad" when Ramesh was diagnosed with pancreatic cancer. Near the end, each friend took a different night of the week to stay with him.

On one of my last shifts, I heard the door open at 3:00 a.m. Ramesh had wandered outside, completely nude, in the middle of January, falling down twice and skinning both knees before I could get him back to the house.

After that, the Squad brought on a couple more members, and we stayed with Ramesh around the clock. He'd asked for Death with Dignity meds but then was afraid to use them, worried there'd be consequences "later."

His hospice nurse had confiscated them the moment Ramesh died. I suppose she was legally obligated.

It wasn't that I wanted to kill myself. But I did want to know I *could*.

Ramesh II looked about now, but there was no obvious place to sit. The bus was "packed" in that every set of seats was occupied by a single person. To sit anywhere, he'd have to sit right next to someone else. Even before the pandemic, people avoided such proximity whenever possible. Now, it felt like groping.

I motioned to the seat beside me.

The man looked at the seat, glanced over at me, surveyed the bus again, and then moved past me to stand by the rear door.

***

I jumped off the 11 at Westlake and ran down the stairs, almost tripping on the last flight. I dashed around the corner, slapped my Orca card against the reader, and grunted as a red light flashed with an accompanying honk informing me I'd been unsuccessful.

The reader broke down regularly. I slapped my card against it three more times before getting the green go-ahead and then raced down one last flight of stairs.

Just as the light rail pulled away.

"Cazzo!"

Trains arrived every ten minutes, so it wasn't the end of the world, but after a long day of work, and after missing my first bus, plus knowing I still had one more bus after light rail, it was damned aggravating.

Every day, I told myself not to take chances. Once, I'd slipped on the stairs and almost fallen on my face. Another time, I'd just been recovering from a bout of plantar fasciitis and risked tearing the tendon again. One day, I was getting over a knee injury, caused solely by sitting on my sofa and crossing one leg over the other while watching *The Undertaker*.

But I simply couldn't resist the pull to go home *now*.

At least I hadn't injured myself today. It was only a matter of watching shoppers and workers and tourists milling about for a few more minutes, talking or texting and puffing out invisible virus particles.

Then the elevator doors opened, and a short, balding man with a white cane came tapping out.

Now *that* was a good-looking man.

He apparently had some level of vision, as he moved directly to where the rear doors of the last car typically opened. He'd be ready when the next train came down from Capitol Hill.

The guy was about fifty, far sexier than I'd been at his age. The thought made me realize that even a blind man would probably not feel attracted to me now. He'd still be able to feel my fat stomach, after all.

The man was a little plump himself, but in a dad bod kind of way, not the granddad bod I inhabited.

I watched as he pulled out a magnifying glass to read a text on his cell phone.

That meant he'd be able to read my phone number if I wrote it in large enough numerals. But I couldn't just thrust a piece of paper at him. I'd have to chat him up first. Yet what would I say?

"Lovely weather we're having down here in the tunnel, isn't it?"

The man turned vaguely toward me. It looked as if his eyes saw mine. I didn't have a follow-up comment, though, and the man turned back to his phone. He probably wasn't even sure I'd been talking to him, so I couldn't be certain I'd been rebuffed.

But I still felt like the idiot I was.

When the train pulled up a few minutes later, the guy moved immediately to the disabled section. That was one of two bench seats in the car. I could sit on the far end of the bench without crowding him, but it felt too stalkerish, so I sat on the first row in the elevated section on the other side of the doors.

I'd already made contact, though, hadn't I? It would be OK now to hand him my phone number on the way out. Assuming he didn't deboard at an earlier stop.

If he never called, at least I'd know I tried.

The guy fell asleep shortly after Columbia City. He was still sleeping as we left Othello. I could hardly wake him up to shove a slip of paper in his pocket.

I could always stay on the train past my stop, of course. He'd surely wake up for his own. I wouldn't need to deboard with him and be all creepy, but I could hand him the slip of paper as he left.

Going even one stop further, though, would add half an hour to my commute.

The man was still sleeping when the train stopped at Rainier Beach. I took one last look and then bolted when the doors opened. If I hurried, I could cross MLK before the Walk sign changed to Don't Walk. That would give me a fighting chance to catch my last bus on time.

If I didn't damage a tendon first.

***

I'd had disturbing dreams most of the previous evening. In one, a Jewish family that spoke almost no English was looking for a specific synagogue, but the only Hebrew word I could remember from college was "shalom." In another, Brigham and I were arguing over whether to sail or fly to Iceland.

The one outright nightmare had been more traditional—me running for the bus, my legs trapped in molasses that smelled like tar.

This morning, I walked down to the stop below mine, pleased to see Tommy already waiting. I felt stupid and predatory, horny and inadequate. Tommy waved, thrusting his hips forward as if fucking. When I reached the bus stop, he took the bag out of my hand and set it on the sidewalk. Then he gave me a bear hug that lasted almost a minute, grinding against me while cars sped by on Renton.

The speed limit was an unrealistic twenty-five on almost every arterial in the city.

When Tommy pulled back, he tapped my crotch lightly. "Gave you a chubby," he said triumphantly. Then he reached for his zipper.

"We can't do that here," I said.

"I'm not shy."

"It's not socially appropriate," I said.

Tommy sighed heavily. "Would you do it in a bar?"

Probably not, I thought. That could also be grounds for arrest. "What bar do you go to?" I asked. A gay bar in White Center had just been torched by an arsonist the week before. Thank God, no one had been inside at the time.

"Bear Trap up on Capitol Hill," he said. "They have a beer bust tonight. Wanna meet me there after work?"

A bear bar. Why hadn't I thought of that? Even with a pandemic, I was going to have to go somewhere and take off my mask sometime if I wanted any type of acceptable human interaction. That was all there was to it.

"Yes," I said. "Yes, I do."

Tommy grabbed me again in a tight hug. This time, he pressed his mask against mine as hard as he could and moaned like Al Parker.

Chapter Three: The Road to Market

Super Super Market Market. "So good it resonates."

I wasn't sure resonating was the same as echoing, but since I wasn't in Marketing, I didn't agonize much over my workplace slogan. I was just grateful to get through another shift and not miss the first bus of my commute.

The 11 bumped into the curb, sending a stray cat scurrying. Everyone on board lurched but no one said anything as the bus continued on.

I couldn't even market myself these days. The last time I'd had my photo taken to renew my driver's license, the employee at the Department of Licensing had shown me the result and asked, apologetically, "You want to try again?"

If my driver's license photo was embarrassing, though, the requisite dick pic was downright mortifying. As I had grown larger over the years, my cock had dwindled from 5 ½ inches to 5 to 4 ½ to 4.

What was there to market?

I hadn't yet put up an ad of my own on any of the gay websites, but when I answered the few for which I "qualified," I almost never received a response. If I did, the correspondence soon stopped when I tried to set a firm time for meeting.

Todd Todd Tillotson Tillotson. “So good you’ll want seconds.”

Even I didn’t believe it.

We passed an elderly woman selling *Real Change* newspapers in front of a vegetable stand. Then the old Alano Club, which had burned several years ago but since been renovated. The place still looked old. But across from it was a new apartment building covered with various shades of glass, mostly yellows, oranges, and greens.

Beside this bit of fresh gentrification was a bail bonds storefront, whose front door hadn’t been cleaned since before I met Brigham.

I hoped the bar was air conditioned. The sun was still blazing even this late in the day. I shielded my eyes from the light.

Then I took a deep breath and pulled the cord. The Bear Trap hadn’t even existed the last time I went to a bar. Socializing with Tommy tonight would be unavoidable, but since he was a regular, perhaps that would work in my favor.

I stepped off the bus and started walking south.

I sure hoped I was wearing the right underwear.

And I really, really hoped I’d have a chance to find out.

***

"Run, old man!"

Tommy held the door for me, preventing the driver from pulling away from the bus stop. I hadn't had anything to drink tonight except seltzer water, and since the only snack I'd had was a protein bar around 8:00, I could feel my glucose dropping. Of course, I couldn't afford a new sensor yet, so I couldn't truly be sure.

Perhaps I was simply tired. It was almost 9:30, after all. Almost bedtime.

Tommy had already made his way to the back row of the bus. He patted the seat beside him and I stumbled my way down the aisle as the bus took off.

"Wanna make out?" he asked. Loudly, of course. There weren't many other passengers, and all of them pretended not to hear. Even the driver managed not to look in his rearview mirror, though Tommy's penetrating voice had surely carried all the way to the front.

The nearest passengers were more than six feet away.

"I did some research," I'd heard a woman on the news claim the day before. "Satanists wear masks and stand six feet apart for their rituals. That can't be a coincidence."

I pulled my mask down, Tommy did the same, and we traded tongues for the next few minutes.

He tasted like beer. Fifteen years since our last kiss. He'd gotten better.

I probably hadn't. Brigham was good at a lot of things, but he hadn't liked kissing. I was way out of practice.

A heavyset white man boarded, followed immediately by a heavyset white woman, both in their forties. The man carried a single bag of groceries. I could see a box of corn flakes and a row of chicken breasts stretching through the thin plastic.

The ban on plastic bags had been lifted during the pandemic.

The woman carried a dachshund, black with brown feet. As soon as the couple sat down in the disabled section, she let the dog begin wandering about the bus on its own. A middle-aged Asian man several rows up sent a glare their way.

"You like it doggy style?" Tommy asked, nodding toward the dachshund.

"I like it any way I can get it," I told him.

Tommy laughed, shaking his head. "I'm not into fucking," he said. "Too messy."

The middle-aged Asian man turned to look back at us. A young black man just three rows up did not. Tommy grabbed my face and pulled me into another kiss.

After a moment, I pulled away. "We can't kiss on the bus," I said, replacing my mask.

Tommy grunted. Then he squeezed my thigh. And copped a feel.

"Do you go to the Bear Trap every Tuesday?" I asked.

He nodded. "Can't go home with anyone, though." He shrugged. "My roommate would get mad."

Tommy had received far more attention than I had this evening, had even introduced me to a couple of guys he knew. But I wasn't forty anymore, so their eyes had quickly returned to him.

Tommy started laughing again.

"What?"

He pointed. The dachshund was pissing in the aisle.

That poor driver. To think that two randy men making out in the back row were his good passengers.

"You into that?" Tommy asked.

"Dogs?"

"Piss."

OMG. Why did he have to speak so loudly?

"Maybe in my younger days," I said, "I'd have given it a shot. Now I just want simple, comfortable sex."

I expected judgment, but Tommy nodded. "Blow jobs are easiest. I stick with that."

The heavyset woman turned, pretending to look for her dog but staring at us instead.

Tommy stopped talking then, thank God, and rested his head on my shoulder. Twenty-five minutes later, I nudged him as we approached our stop. He descended first and then offered his hand to help me down. I wasn't *that* decrepit, but I accepted. The sidewalk here was dark, shielded from a streetlight by the low branches of a redwood.

Tommy began unzipping even before the bus pulled off.

"We can't do this in public," I said.

"Not even at night?"

"Nope."

He didn't ask to come to my place, and I didn't offer. I just slapped him a farewell on the shoulder.

Tommy grunted again. "We'll, *I'm* going to beat off. Will you at least watch?"

A car flew by on Renton, but the driver was looking at her cell phone, not peering into the shadows beside the road. I didn't respond, but since I didn't move away, Tommy extracted his dick and started fondling himself. Hardly a minute later, I could hear his breathing change.

"Catch it," I whispered.

A few seconds later, he issued a huge, *loud* sigh the neighbors inside the nearest house could probably hear. I reached over for Tommy's hand and lifted it to my face. The smell was intoxicating. But I couldn't help thinking of all the things he must have touched since he last washed his hands.

"Wipe your cum off on my pants," I told him, guiding his palm to my crotch.

He giggled and wiped. And wiped. After all, we didn't want to make a mess.

Tommy kissed me one last time and headed off down a side street, while I continued up the hill.

How liberating, I thought, needing to worry about STDs again.

***

The only thing worse than running an errand on my day off was doing it on a workday. So I trudged up the hill and around the corner to the bus stop on Renton. The bus wasn't due until 9:00 but sometimes drivers came early, so I was there by 8:52.

The bus pulled up at 9:04. I wiped the sweat from my forehead, the sun already hot.

Brigham used to take care of errands like this for me, but I'd sold his Spark a month after he was killed. Now if I wanted to dispose of my insulin needles, I needed to carry them to an approved drop-off location. The nearest was in Othello Park.

Fortunately, that was just a single bus ride away.

A few blocks further down, I watched a black woman and her pre-teen son descend from their porch and cross Renton to bring a bag of drinks to some of the homeless folks living in their cars.

Along MLK, I watched the world flow past the window—a nail salon and then a car wash and a storefront offering CNA Certificate Classes.

I hopped off the bus and started walking east. Just two blocks down was the park. I'd participated in a Black Lives

Matter protest here a week after the hit and run, carrying a sign that read "LGBTQ for BLM." The other side read "Black Trans Lives Matter." It was the last weekend in June, after all.

I remembered how the white and other non-black folks formed human walls along both sides and the rear of the black marchers, hoping to offer a buffer against counterprotesters. A young white man on a bicycle had ridden back and forth, telling us, "Remember why you're here," to bolster our courage.

The sharps drop box sat next to the bathroom on the edge of the park. I pulled down the lid, much like a neighborhood mailbox, and squeezed my first sharps container inside.

Ker-plunk!

I then squeezed in my second sharps container.

Plunk!

A year's worth of needles.

It was easier now to continue on to Rainier Avenue than backtrack and catch the 106. Far too much trouble to cross MLK at Othello. Heading to Rainier, I wouldn't have to cross a single major intersection.

Someone had posted a "Stop Asian Hate" sign in their living room window and a "Real Rent Duwamish" sign in their front yard.

A Latina teenager pushed a baby stroller past me, avoiding eye contact.

Waiting at the bus stop in front of the gas station on Rainier, I felt a rush of adrenalin when I saw the 7 Prentice approaching. The good 7. I'd be back home less than forty-five minutes after leaving the house.

Victory!

But after passing the community center, the driver pulled into the left lane.

"This is the Prentice!" I called out.

The driver didn't respond, of course. The few passengers left didn't even turn to look at me. I gritted my teeth as the bus rounded the corner onto Henderson and parked in front of the dollar store at the end of the regular 7's route.

While it wasn't the worst thing a bus driver had ever done to me, I still felt robbed. I jogged to the corner just as the Walk sign came on and kept jogging, feeling only a slight twinge in my knee. Maybe this could still be a victory.

But no 106 came from the direction of MLK. Two more 7's came and parked behind the bus I'd arrived on.

An elderly black man in a wrinkled suit shuffled by. A heavyset mixed-race girl chewing gum passed in the opposite direction, tossing a look of disdain my way.

A few minutes later, I saw a 7 Prentice heading toward me, staying in the correct lane.

Thank God.

I climbed on board and finally let my guard down. I could never relax until I knew I was really and truly on the last leg of the journey.

We drove past a waterfront condo under construction and turned up the hill past the auto supply store. A few weeks ago, a Filipino teen a block away had been shot and killed when he opened his front door around 11:00 at night.

Just before we turned onto 62nd, a spectacular vista, Lake Washington with hills and mountains beyond, came into view. It took longer to get home on the 7 Prentice than the 106, but that view was always restorative.

I pulled the cord near the top of the hill and climbed down when the driver opened the door. Hardly any traffic on the back streets. A breathtaking redwood the width of a car between two houses. Yellow day lilies blooming in yards.

And a tiny traffic island covered in California poppies. Where a man watering them was killed shortly after Brigham and I moved to the neighborhood.

Turning onto my block, I started walking uphill again. When I reached my porch, I looked at my watch. 10:02.

An hour and ten minutes. It could have been worse. I still had plenty of time to read before the afternoon sun made the porch unbearable.

Something light and fun today. Perhaps a book I'd ordered months ago, *The Ghost Wore Yellow Socks*.

***

"You'd look younger if you lost some weight." The white man, fiftyish, made an exaggerated left-to-right movement with his head while evaluating me horizontally. "A *lot* of weight." We were waiting at the light rail station on Capitol Hill. The next train heading south was due "in two minutes."

It had been due in two minutes for five minutes now.

"I appreciate the concern," I said. I'd never seen the man before. I gathered he was gay, given the bitchy tone, but he wouldn't have been my type regardless of his disinterest.

Bitchy only looked good on people in TV shows.

"Since we're giving out free advice," I continued, "*you'd* look a lot smarter if you kept your mouth shut."

Two young white men nearby laughed. "Yeah," one of them joined in, "but he can't give you a blow job with his mouth closed."

"I don't want to give him a blow job!" the fifty-year-old protested.

"Then why do you care what he looks like?" the young man responded, jerking a thumb in my direction.

A visible invisible man.

The fifty-year-old marched off to another part of the platform, and the two young men nodded at me. "Thank you?" I said.

"I used to be fat, too," the second young man told me. "This guy—" He patted his boyfriend's shoulder. "—helped me get in shape."

"Get an exercise bike," the other young man said. "And pedal while you're watching porn."

"Slow at first and then faster and faster and..."

A cool rush of wind started gathering on the platform, indicating the train was finally approaching. Once on board and seated, I started looking up stationary bicycles. That suggestion didn't sound half bad.

The two young men sat half a car away, and I watched them talking and laughing with one another as we moved through the tunnel.

Happiness by proxy.

Chapter Four: A Fork in the Road

Three rides in a row had gone smoothly, practically unheard of. There was always someone refusing to wear a mask, of course, but they'd remained several rows away. And they weren't coughing.

Still, I was dreading my morning commute today more for its destination. I'd be working with Gail, and she could always work my last nerve.

After thoroughly shredding the penultimate one.

While Gail and I technically had the same job title, she acted as assistant supervisor and seemed to get the perks of management without the responsibility. She routinely called in sick at the last minute. Twice last year, she'd called to say she thought she had COVID. I'd lost two weeks of hours self-quarantining, only to hear her saying later to another coworker that both times she'd just needed to take a mental health day.

It clearly hadn't served its function.

Gail had also taken off for the deaths of six grandparents, who'd all died of COVID. Our supervisor didn't remember that two of those grandparents had died before the pandemic as well.

I hopped off the 106 at Mount Baker. The back doors opened onto a tree, so I squeezed around it to reach the sidewalk.

A homeless black man stood near the ATM, cursing the world. People walked past as if he didn't exist.

I debated taking the 48, just to get away from the transit center faster, but I held on for the 8, watching as a black woman in short shorts handed a piece of paper to a man boarding the 7. She then approached a man getting off at the rear, handing him a piece of paper as well.

I really needed to polish my marketing skills.

A siren blared from the fire station a couple of blocks away. I plugged my ears as the engine drove past. The 8 came a few minutes later, and I found a seat with only partial access to a window, hoping to block some of the sun. I wiped the sweat from around my eyes with my sleeves.

Several bushes along this stretch, even a few trees, had died from lack of water so far this summer. And this part of the state was only considered "abnormally dry." Much of the rest was in "moderate," "severe," or "extreme" drought, with almost half of Washington now suffering "exceptional" drought.

A mixed-race woman with two black kids boarded. Neither child could have been over five, but both were appropriately masked.

I knew I wasn't supposed to note color or ethnicity, but of course I did, just like everyone else. I didn't see "a woman with two kids." I saw color. There was no point in pretending. And I was certain I made biased assumptions and judgments all the time. I simply made an effort to reevaluate, accept correction and do a tiny bit better the next day.

Once in a great while, I even succeeded.

The Central District had been historically black, and large parts of it still were, but even larger sections had gentrified, the anchor grocery transformed into condos. We passed a home proudly displaying its "12" flag. A little library stood amongst dead weeds in front of another home. And a block beyond that, I mourned a 45-foot dead cedar, rust-colored from bottom to top.

In the next block, I experienced a rare epiphany—the portable toilet I'd seen in the front yard of a modest home for months had no reason for being there. No construction seemed to be going on at that address or anywhere nearby.

Was this the owner's idea of a political statement? An art installation?

Perhaps performance art?

Surely, the owner wasn't creating his own bathroom sex opportunities, was he? More likely there was nothing salacious about it at all. Maybe she or he was simply providing a public service for the homeless folks in the area.

The idea made me smile.

The bus stopped in front of a grocery discount store. I did a lot of my own shopping here rather than at Super

Super Market Market. I didn't earn enough to pay full price.

And without Brigham's income…

An elderly white man boarded, dragging his shopping cart. It caught on the door, but rather than back up and aim better, he began yelling at the driver. His mask was down below his nose, so no one approached to help.

The driver didn't even look in his direction, just waited patiently until the guy finally figured out how to dislodge the cart. As soon as he sat down, the driver closed the doors and started off again.

The man's cart rolled two inches and bumped against an empty seat.

"I'm gonna report you!" The man waved his fist toward the front of the bus.

I jotted a note to go online during my break and commend the driver for his professionalism.

I wondered how many drivers stuck their tongues out underneath their masks.

"This is my stop!" I yelled a few moments later when it became clear the driver hadn't heard the bell.

He screeched to a halt and opened the rear doors. "Sorry!" he shouted into his rearview mirror.

"No problem." I'd try to zone out, too, in his position.

***

"Honk!"

"Honk!"

"Honk!

"Honk!"

The damn card reader still wasn't working. I hurried down the last flight of stairs and over to the card reader beside the platform. I'd left work half an hour earlier and still had both the light rail and another bus ahead of me. Commuting was like a second, part-time job.

With no chance of promotion.

How had Brigham and I ever managed to spend any quality time together? He'd have dinner waiting for me when I walked in the door, I'd wash dishes afterward, and then we'd sit down to watch an hour of MHz. *Imma Tataranni*, perhaps, or *La Porta Rossa*, or *The Bastards of Pizzofalcone*.

Bastards was starting its second season now.

More often than not, Brigham would fall asleep on the sofa holding my hand while I watched the remainder of the show by myself. These days, I sometimes held onto one of his shirts while I watched.

I scanned the platform for the cute blind man. He wasn't there today, but woof! *That* guy looked just like the German actor in *Murder by the Lake*.

I'd studied French in high school, hoping I'd be sent to France or Quebec, and I'd made sure to keep up my Italian since returning from my mission. Maybe it was time to try learning some Germanic languages.

If only their words didn't have so many syllables!

While I was attempting not to stare at the detective's doppelgänger, I heard a tap beside me. The cute blind man had just stepped off the elevator. Whoo hoo!

The train pulled up before I could work up the nerve to say hi, and I still didn't want to make the guy uncomfortable by sitting too close. Once I found my own seat, I opened my wallet and pulled out the paper with my name and number. I was going to give it to him today, even if he was sleeping. I'd wake him up. I would.

Several tourists, all white, boarded at the University Street station, dragging huge suitcases. Not a single one in the group wore a mask.

"Stronzi," I muttered out loud, but softly because I didn't want the cute guy to think I was a nut.

I forced myself to look out the window.

At Stadium station, several bus drivers deboarded, apparently to do paperwork or pick up a bus across the street. A handful of other folks dressed in Mariners gear stepped off as well. In the Beacon Hill tunnel, I watched as we zoomed past huge, lighted playing cards installed along the walls. An ace, a king, a queen.

The tourists were still blathering on. "People are so rude here." Apparently, the put upon tourists had been asked more than a few times to wear masks and seemed to find this unbearable. Once we were down on MLK, I tried harder to ignore them, but they were so *loud*.

Were they related to Tommy?

One of the men was laughing about the Black Lives Matter mural in the middle of Pine Street. "The police station is still all covered with grates," the man scoffed. "*I'll* never come back here again."

"From your mouth to God's ears."

Damn it. I'd spoken out loud. But I was still looking out the window and pretended I hadn't heard a sound.

After we passed Othello, I stole a peek at the cute blind man. He must have shaved the little bit of hair he did have. I felt an almost irresistible urge to lick his scalp. And his neck. And…

Thank God he wasn't sleeping today. But he was on his phone. I strained to hear him through the onslaught of tourist decibels. The guy was probably partnered and monogamous.

Did he just say "trabajo"? "Machaca"?

Maybe we could watch *Felix* together. Only he probably didn't watch much TV, even if he could understand it.

Or was I making assumptions? It wouldn't hurt to ask.

But he was still on the phone when the train stopped at Rainier Beach. And the tourists were still sending shock waves through the air. Their noise *hurt*.

I stepped off the train with my phone number still in my hand. "Porca la Madonna!" I slapped myself for my cowardice, causing a white woman to move to the other side of the platform.

I stood impatiently for over three minutes beside a black woman wearing a khimar and an Asian teen casually sipping bubble tea while we waited for the Walk sign to light up. By then, I'd missed the 106. But the 107 should be there soon. That would get me halfway up the hill. I could walk the rest of the way from there. It wasn't as if I didn't have fat to burn.

***

Earbud day.

I kept my eyes closed aboard the train, easy to keep track of the stops without looking, though I peeked every few minutes just to make sure.

The cute Latino wasn't on board today, his day off perhaps, or maybe he'd caught an earlier train or was running a few minutes late. Any opportunity to reach out to him struck me as dangerously fragile and fleeting.

Had I already flubbed my last chance?

I listened to Maroon 5 singing "Animal."

And Train singing "Drive By."

Pink singing "Walk Me Home."

Imagine Dragons singing, "Demons."

But even the soothing voice of George Ezra singing "Budapest" couldn't block out the sound of a drunk—or crazy—or drunk and crazy—man singing at the top of his lungs on the far end of the car.

The only word I could make out was “Fuck,” used in almost every sentence.

It didn’t sound like a Top Ten hit. But then, I wasn’t pop culture savvy anymore.

***

I watched three young hikers board the shuttle to Mt. Si, an Asian woman and two white men.

Brigham and I had hiked up there a few times ourselves. Most of our trips the last few years, though, consisted in riding the ferry to Bainbridge and back, inexpensive but still thrilling, usually on my birthday. He liked to go to the baths alone on his. For our anniversary, we’d pack a simple picnic and eat at the base of a giant sequoia in the Arboretum.

A man sleeping on the bench at Bay 2 suddenly awoke and vomited onto the pavement. A nearby crow pecking at something on the sidewalk flew off. A middle-aged white man with unkempt hair walked by, wearing a T-shirt with the words “Freedom isn’t free” superimposed over an American flag.

In the distance, I admired Mt. Rainier, the smoke from the wildfires blowing away from the Sound today. A woman had fallen through an ice bridge on the volcano the previous week and been killed, the temperatures in the northwest exceptionally warm all month.

I’d seen a report about wildfires in Sardinia on BBC News. I’d worked in Cagliari for three months. Brigham had served in Sassari for two.

Kevin, my last senior companion back in Rome One, had been a flight attendant the past forty years. Now that restrictions were lifting, he'd resumed his route to Rome and had sent me a video of our old neighborhood along Via Casilina, poor and occupied these days by Syrian and African immigrants. Kevin had been too nervous to get off the tram and explore.

I wondered what he'd think of south Seattle.

The driver revved the engine on the 8 when she finished her break. Then she turned on the "Seattle Center" sign and pulled around the far end of the transit center lot. I was already waiting right where I knew the doors would open.

But I saw a tiny Filipina woman hovering near the trash can and waved her on board first.

***

I braced against the seat in front of me as the train screeched to a halt. Most of the passengers peered out the windows with mild curiosity. We weren't at a station, not even at an intersection. From the rear of the third car, I couldn't see what was happening up front, but it was clearly not good.

Occasionally, light rail struck a car crossing the tracks at the wrong time. Every once in a great while, the train struck a pedestrian.

Within moments, faint sirens in the distance quickly grew louder.

Three Asian teenagers talked excitedly into their phones. Two tourist couples, both white, surrounded by suitcases on opposite ends of the car, began worrying loudly they'd miss their flight. At least they were wearing masks.

"We are experiencing a service delay," a recorded female voice spoke over the intercom. "The train will be moving shortly. We apologize for the delay."

The sound was muffled and scratchy, and I felt for those whose primary language wasn't English. Too bad the blind Latino wasn't aboard today. The fuzzy recording would have given me a reason to talk to him.

Five minutes passed, and we still hadn't moved. Traffic was backing up on MLK's northbound lanes.

One of the tourists was pacing back and forth between the doors closest to me, looking at his watch. His wife was on the phone.

A young Indian man, not quite thirty, seemed oblivious to the tension. He chatted happily with a Chinese woman of similar age. The man wore skinny slacks, a white button-down shirt with the sleeves rolled up, and brightly colored, striped socks. The young woman wore a red dress partially covered by a black leather jacket. They were both masked.

I knew they were on a date because they both laughed at everything the other said.

"We killed a man!" The wife of the pacer held her phone out for her husband to see. "Some idiot walked right in front of the train. He's going to ruin everything!"

I remembered the old woman we'd hit on a commuter train near Castel Gandolfo.

I wondered if this pedestrian had also been too old to cross the tracks quickly. Perhaps he was visually impaired. Or hard of hearing.

Or maybe he'd deliberately thrown himself in front of the train. The eviction moratorium was expiring in a few days.

I tried not to imagine the scene two and a half cars ahead of us, feeling a case of Haley Joel Osment coming on. I kept seeing Brigham the night we joined the CHOP protest. He was wearing his Che T-shirt.

I'd been more worried than Brigham. Vendors were selling hot dogs and burritos. Families brought children in strollers. But it was impossible not to see video of rubber bullets and police beatings at protests across the country. Every evening, we watched officers tase journalists for no reason, push old men down in the street, kick pregnant women, even pepper spray six-year-olds.

As a white man, it was easy to forget those long months of protests a year later.

Another protester that night had pushed me out of the way when the SUV aimed for us. I'd skinned my elbow but was otherwise unharmed.

Brigham's left pants leg was covered in blood. He was bleeding from his scalp, too.

I wanted to give him a priesthood blessing.

I wanted him to wake up.

I wanted to tell him everything was going to be OK.

A transit employee knocked on the doors of our car before opening them and directing everyone out. Another employee led us across the southbound lanes of MLK, where two buses had arrived to carry passengers to stops farther down the line.

I headed for Rainier instead, only five blocks away, and waited for the 7. If I was lucky, it would be the 7 Prentice.

And if I was really, really lucky, it would actually complete its route.

Chapter Five: The Long and Winding Road

The bus pulled to the curb and the doors opened. "Stop fucking with the disabled!" A man who appeared able-bodied shook his fist at the driver and stepped off the bus, stalking away and slapping the side of the bus shelter.

***

My day off, but I was still standing beside the bus stop at 8:30. Getting an early start was the only way to squeeze in several chores on one outing and still have part of the day left to enjoy. I'd walked down to Rainier to get in a little exercise and was now sweating in the quickly developing heat.

A young black couple pushing a baby stroller joined me at the bus stop. "I gotta pee," the woman announced. She walked behind the shelter, still in view of anyone at the gas station on the other side, and squatted.

After she returned, the young man walked behind the shelter and unzipped.

The family that pees together…

The woman gave the last bite of her candy bar to their toddler and then threw the wrapper on the ground, ignoring the trash can two feet away.

A 7 rounded the corner a moment later. I jumped on, lifting the disability bench to make room for the stroller, and then moved deeper into the bus.

A man covered in garbage bags huddled against a window. Two rows further back, a young Asian twink with purple hair bobbed his head to the music in his earbuds. The row behind him was empty, and I paused.

Was that a peeled fig on the seat?

I kept walking and finally found a spot that felt safe enough to sit for twenty minutes.

We passed a Vietnamese restaurant and a teriyaki place and several African restaurants and markets. I noticed a few bikes and scooters abandoned on sidewalks. They were available for rent and I supposed served a useful function, though I couldn't imagine many places I'd go where I wouldn't be carrying something rendering those modes of transportation inadequate.

I stepped off the bus north of Columbia City and walked half a block to the post office, where I mailed a book of stories and poems about mental health recovery to a friend in Utah. Makenna was bipolar but on meds and doing well.

I caught myself picking at the skin on my forearm and gave myself a slap.

I was headed to the main commercial area of Columbia City next, only a ten-minute walk, so I started heading south. Since we were outdoors, most pedestrians were maskless, but I kept mine on because removing it meant storing the thing somewhere it would stay clean.

A middle-aged Asian woman strolling in my direction wore a mask printed with Hokusai's Great Wave woodcut.

Floods in Belgium and Germany had left at least 195 people dead.

A friend of mine was moving from San Francisco out to wine country, retired and wanting some peace. It was impossible not to worry about Debryant's new home burning down within the next few years, but what was there to do? No place seemed safe anymore.

Debryant had sent me $60 for my sixtieth birthday last week. I'd donated it all to RIP Medical Debt.

At the clinic in Columbia City, I pulled a number and waited for my turn at the lab, time for my A1C, lipid panel, and viral load. Weight gain was a common side effect of three of the prescriptions I'd been on for years. I hated these fasting labs, though if my doctor was smart, he'd order them monthly and schedule the blood draw for mid-afternoon. Yes, it would cost them money, but it would get me used to a full day of intermittent fasting on a regular basis, and that had to be cost efficient in the long run. It wasn't as if I was completely powerless against the meds.

"Mr. Tillotson," the phlebotomist said after reviewing my file, "your doctor hasn't ordered a lipid panel. But we can go ahead with the other labs."

Damn. I should have checked before leaving the house. I remembered distinctly Dr. Kamdar saying he was ordering the lipid panel.

But then, we'd also done a cognitive test, Trump's "Person Woman Man Camera TV" made famous by Sarah Cooper. And I hadn't done as well as the former president.

"Oh, I think I'll just wait and do it all with one stick. I'm sorry to take up your time."

While I was at the clinic, though, I figured I might as well pick up a new sharps container. But…they were all out.

I had a half hour to kill before my dental appointment a couple of blocks over. The bus bench was sticky, so I just strolled around the block again and again. Might as well make use of the fasting.

In the past, I'd have called Brigham. Seven years older than me, he was already retired. Even if he was busy on a project, he'd pick up the phone and we'd practice our Italian. We'd talk about our plans for the day or the news or what we might have for dinner. Mostly, though, we spoke Italian to reminisce.

"Ti ricordo il Metro a Roma?" he asked during one of our last conversations. I easily noticed his many errors while missing my own.

"Sì," I'd replied. "Siamo andati spesso a Cinecittà." I'd had such a crush on a straight guy who worked at the studio. Aldo had been fully aware and seemed amused. He was a capoelettricista but still had a head shot he gifted me on our last visit, when I told him I was being transferred to Sardinia.

For our first anniversary, Brigham had commissioned one of our neighbors, a straight black woman, to paint a larger version of the photo, which he then had framed for me.

"Let's hang it in the bedroom," Brigham had suggested. "That way you won't even have to close your eyes when you want to pretend you're with someone else."

Fair was fair. He had a photo of one of his hunkiest exes on the bedside table next to his lube drawer.

I'd tried for years to talk Brigham into letting me arrange a professional photo shoot to get a quality nude portrait of him. He'd been beautiful up to the very end. But he thought I was teasing every time I said, "Woof!"

I realized I'd stopped walking and was staring at a boarded up restaurant that hadn't been one of the survivors.

At the dental clinic, I felt downright criminal removing my mask for the cleaning. The hygienist wore both a mask and a face shield and talked non-stop during the procedure. "These anti-vaxxers are driving me crazy," she said. "When I started college, I had to get two measles boosters. I thought it was stupid to need two, but the school required it, and I did it. That's what you do. You suck up the inconvenience and act like an adult."

The scaler slipped and cut into my gums, and I grunted.

"Oops." The hygienist pressed some cotton gauze against my gums and held it there for almost a minute as she kept talking. But I was happy to be in the chair. Human interaction felt wonderful.

Finally, though, we were done, and I crossed the street to wait for a 7 to take me back to Rainier Beach. I actually clapped when the 7 Prentice showed up instead.

And then the driver turned early and parked in front of the dollar store, so I had to cross the street again and wait for the 106. I could see the one I'd just missed heading away up the hill. A 107 came, which I decided not to take, then another 107 fifteen minutes later. Two more 7's turned onto Henderson. And finally, a 106 came around the corner.

I stepped over a laundry bag in the aisle and stood by the rear exit, arriving back at the house just before 1:45. The entire day had felt like one long commute, the tasks and chores part of the ride, not independent in any way.

It was *impossible* to see them as separate, when every tiny delay had me reviewing bus schedules in my head, when every failure reminded me I'd have to make the same miserable trip again.

I exhaled in relief when I closed the front door.

But I'd forgotten to pick up eggs, one of the few things I could eat these days. Boiled for a snack at work, scrambled or fried for dinner while watching MHz.

"Dannazione!"

I opened the door and headed back for the bus stop.

***

"Why is Santa wearing a mask?" The young boy, around seven, pointed as I walked down the aisle. Fortunately, the boy and his mother were also wearing masks. Hers projected out three inches from her face and was covered with topographic contour lines as if her nose were a mountain being mapped. The boy's mask displayed brightly colored dinosaurs. I was jealous.

The woman pulled her son's pointing hand away, shaking her head in an apology to me.

Christmas in July, I supposed. We all needed Hallmark these days.

Hunter Burke was hot.

"My elves haven't been vaccinated yet," I told the boy. "And some of them are immunocompromised."

I'd have made such a good father.

I kept walking until I reached the next to last row of the bus. I didn't want to get caught up in a conversation about toymaking, and I could hardly engage the boy in promises of sweaters and socks, much less about gifting him the book I'd just finished, *Up in the Air*.

A middle-aged black woman across the aisle looked at me with a twinkle in her eyes. She was masked, too, but I imagined a smile beneath it. "No one ever asks that of Mrs. Claus," she said, patting her stomach.

I almost smiled back, despite knowing she couldn't see mine, either, but she followed her comment with one far less funny. "We get asked about our syrup."

***

My blood pressure medication gave me a morning cough, so I tried to wake up two hours earlier than I "needed" to. That usually offered my body time to calm down and not scare other passengers on the bus.

Of course, the side effect of the medication still scared *me*. Even though I'd had this morning cough for a few years already, every morning since the pandemic began, I woke up wondering, "Oh my God, is this really *it* today?"

I remembered thinking back when I seroconverted that I simply had a bad cold or the flu like Richard had experienced a few weeks earlier.

But I knew what I was dealing with now. A couple of hours after waking up, my cough would subside and I'd feel safe enough to venture out of the house.

The driver with the shaved head and longish white beard opened the door to let me board. One stop later, Tommy boarded the bus and sat beside me, squeezing my thigh in greeting.

"I got called a faggot at work," he announced. The sound echoed through the bus.

"I'm sorry to hear that."

"Yeah, this woman called me a faggot and then called my supervisor an N-word."

Only Tommy didn't say "N-word." He said the real thing. Loudly. While I tried frantically to think what to do, Tommy continued with his story, repeating again and again how the incident had evolved, each time embellishing the story with conflicting details. The one consistent part of the story was the LOUD use of epithets.

"Tommy," I finally said, far too late, "you can't say those words."

"But—"

"Not even if you're quoting someone."

"But—"

"It's not socially acceptable."

He grunted.

"You're going to have to trust me on this." I squeezed his thigh, and he grabbed my crotch in return.

Then we reached his stop. "You have a good day," I said. Tommy nodded and continued on to work.

A middle-aged Latino who'd just boarded started coughing. He was wearing a mask. That is, he wore a mask *until* he started coughing. Then he removed it as if to keep it clean. He put it back on but then a few moments later when he felt a sneeze coming on, he pulled it off once more.

Last night on the news, I'd seen clips showing folks claiming at hearings that the vaccine caused people to become magnetic, that women who were merely in the same room as someone who'd been vaccinated were mysteriously rendered infertile.

We passed a sandwich shop, and a commercial psychic, and a community garden.

Perhaps I should try out the Bear Trap again tonight, I thought. It was Monday, and Tommy probably wouldn't be there until Tuesday. It was difficult to be patient when you didn't feel you had much time left.

Chapter Six: My Address Is Bus Shelter 412

Drunk bears were not very appealing. Even non-drunk bears who looked at me like I'd escaped a traveling circus didn't do much for me. I expected I was imagining most of their judgment, but while I found some of the men at Bear Trap unattractive, many of them looked rather hot, even those who were bigger than I was.

It was just hard not to feel repulsive even among other bears.

I kept a rubber band around both wrists now and tried to snap myself whenever I started picking at my skin. It seemed to be working. Sometimes.

***

The only way to get my colonoscopy was to forgo the sedation. Otherwise, I wasn't permitted to take the bus home. I hadn't had a great many friends before getting together with Brigham, and over the years, most of us had drifted apart. Brigham had kept up with his friends more easily because he had the car, but with work and wanting to spend time with Brigham and *not* wanting any additional time on the bus, I eventually lost most of my own.

There was no one to ask to come with me to the hospital. I couldn't even check in at the reception desk without proof of chauffeur.

A young, white woman boarded the 8 and sat on one of the seats facing sideways just in front of the accordion section of the articulated bus, obediently wearing her mask.

Under her nose, as if she considered it sunblock for her lips and chin.

She pulled out her Bible and began to read.

A few stops later, another white woman boarded. Her clothes were dirty, and she carried an empty, filthy bird cage without a bird. But she was masked.

I felt a gurgle deep in my gut and made a mental note to stop in the bathroom before checking in, even if by this point it was just gas.

I probably shouldn't have waited so long for my first colonoscopy. Sixty was pushing it. But I'd heard terrible warnings, like they gave you a date rape drug so you forgot the procedure.

Of course, forgetting wasn't the same as not experiencing. If it was traumatic, I'd still have to endure it in real time, even if I forgot later that I'd done so.

And goddamn if I didn't hate needles. Blood draws were bad enough. And insulin needles were tiny. But IVs…those things *hurt*!

I'd called ahead of time to explain I couldn't get a ride and was told the only way I could proceed with the appointment was to waive sedation. Since that also meant waiving the IV, I thought it a fair trade.

Unless it meant I didn't get the date rape drug and would be forever traumatized by the experience.

Scanning the other men on the bus, I wished I had a date today worth remembering.

A white guy who might have been FTM stumbled and spilled his soda in the aisle. He tried, unsuccessfully, to kick the pooled liquid underneath a seat. He had a sexy goatee but was just way too young, probably in his twenties.

Perhaps if I lived to seventy…

The 8 dropped me off a block from the building I needed. A group of homeless women across the street sat on a park bench in a tiny area blocked off by yellow tape and orange netting, neither a match for tired folks who just wanted to sit down.

***

The colonoscopy was the closest I'd come to sex in two years.

Of course, I couldn't tell the doctor that. Or the nurse who wheeled me back to my clothes, praising me for being "a good boy."

I'd never stopped feeling attracted to Brigham, but I couldn't blame him for losing his sexual interest in me. I was fat even before he died, and I'd gained ten pounds in the months immediately after.

The only uncomfortable part of the day's procedure was the doctor shoving his fingers into my asshole to lube me up before inserting the scope. Clearly a straight man who'd never been pegged.

The world looked clean and fresh on my way out of the hospital. Even the homeless women seemed happy.

And I hadn't had any medication at all.

Once the scope itself was in, things had gone smoothly, some minor discomfort because the doctor was pumping me full of CO_2, but other than that, I had a rather good time. I watched images of my sparkling clean colon on the monitor, wanting so badly to take advantage of its availability after we finished by asking all the male staff on the unit into the room.

"Hey, guys, gather round..." Someone should do a cover of James Taylor's song using masculine words and pronouns.

I'd been riding my stationary bike religiously and had lost an entire pound and a half. Laughable, I suppose, but I wasn't even embarrassed to have the staff looking at the ass of a fat man.

The only close call had been when the nurse wanted to check my glucose before we started. "I checked it in the waiting room," I said. "It's 99." I was lying, but I got out of the finger stick.

Rather than take the 8 back, I walked down the hill to the light rail station on Broadway. I could feel wind pushing up out of the ground but of course couldn't tell which of the two trains was approaching, so I ran down the escalators hoping for the best.

Both trains were at the station. I dodged around several riders who were letting the escalator do the work for them and dashed through the doors just two seconds before they closed.

Now I was huffing and puffing, and even with my mask on, I expected the other riders were irritated. No heavy breathing allowed during a pandemic!

I found a seat near the back of the car and slid next to the window. But I needn't have worried about others feeling annoyed with me. A heavyset white couple in the middle of the car drew everyone's attention instead. The man's mask was below his nose in that ever more popular fashion while the woman's covered her nose properly. The problem was that whenever she responded to something the man said, she pinched the fabric on her mask and pulled it away a couple of inches from her face, replacing it after she finished speaking.

Kind of like a man ejaculating in spurts, replacing the condom only between spurts while letting his cum shoot free during the critical parts of the act.

At least I wasn't going to die of colon cancer. Not anytime soon, anyway. Turned out I had two polyps, both about the size of sesame seeds. Though they'd been sent off to the lab, it was unlikely either was cancerous.

Even better news was that because I did have polyps, I needed to come back for another colonoscopy in two years.

It was better than lowering myself onto a black butt plug on the edge of my tub.

I'd watched the doctor cut the polyps out and could see blood on the screen but because there were no pain receptors up there, it had not been stressful.

Had people been lying about the date rape drug?

I dozed until we came out of the Beacon Hill tunnel. A white man lay at the top of the stairs at Mount Baker.

We passed an Asian market, a cannabis shop, something boarded up and covered with graffiti, and a bus stop where a black woman in a very short dress davened as if at the Wailing Wall.

My doctor had diagnosed diverticulosis, which he said was both common and incurable, only a problem if it became diverticulitis.

"I volunteered to do a report on that in high school health class," I told him.

He hadn't registered the comment, but a nurse on the other side of the room snickered.

I decided to walk from the light rail station up the hill to my place, twenty-five minutes on a good day, but I was strolling casually, unconcerned about the time. The weather was cooler today, lower eighties, with a few spotty clouds offering moments of shade. And it was so nice to use a sick day to get out of work.

I meandered up Renton, this lower stretch all trees and no houses. But plenty of campers, a couple of 18-wheeler cabs, and a handful of cars people were living in. A heavyset white woman leaned against her car, smoking a cigarette. Half a block further up, a middle-aged white man sat in the door of his truck cab, staring at the ground.

I knew it was inappropriate. I *knew* it. But he looked so down I thought even I might have something worth offering.

"Hey," I said.

"Hey."

"Anything I can do to help relieve some stress?" Sheesh.

The man's dull expression reminded me of the images I'd seen of poor children in Africa with flies all over their faces and no energy to brush them away. "Got $80,000 to pay my wife's medical bills?"

There wasn't even any pain in his face. And not much despair. Only…emptiness. "I'm sorry," I said. "I don't. Is she OK?"

He shook his head. "Not anymore."

I couldn't think of anything to say and was just about to start walking again when I decided to ask one last question. "You need a place to do your laundry?" I pointed up the hill. "I can give you my phone number and arrange to be home when you need to stop by." I thought a second. "You can take a shower when you want, too."

The man's eyes narrowed.

"No strings attached," I said.

A shower and a washing machine were more useful than a clean colon any day. And I had a lovely blue dildo I could use on myself when I got home. No manipulative human behavior required.

The man held out his hand, and I pulled a slip of paper from my pocket to write down my number.

***

The black guy who hung around the ATM next to the Mount Baker Transit Center was yelling at the world. Most people walked past or dodged him without making eye contact, but one elderly Asian woman pulled some individually wrapped pieces of candy from a bag she was carrying and handed them to him.

He took the candies without acknowledging her, popped one in his mouth, and leaned against the bus shelter to suck on it.

Chapter Seven: Detours

On the front lawn of a church were two dozen handmade signs, each bearing the name of a black man or woman killed by the police. In the middle of the field was a larger sign, "You Are Here," beside the outline of a head and neck, with a big red dot in the center of the forehead.

***

Earbud day.

I was in a reasonably good mood for a change. I'd even caught myself humming earlier that morning while trimming my nose hairs.

Though my music was randomized, the AI involved seemed to recognize my mood and issued appropriate offerings.

Panic! At the Disco expressed "High Hopes."

Beyoncé trilled "Halo."

Adele belted out "Set Fire to the Rain."

And Kelly Clarkson celebrated being "Broken and Beautiful."

Four police cars zoomed past the bus only a few meters apart. I could also hear, and soon see, a police helicopter overhead.

Folks on the sidewalk seemed oblivious. A couple headed into a noodle shop, dragging a toddler behind them. Two teens chatted in front of a Polynesian grocery. And a man exited a store whose sign was printed in lettering I couldn't identify.

Lady Gaga danced more than sang "Stupid Love," but I could remember the video as I listened. I liked the fat black woman.

I almost still felt good by the time I reached my stop.

***

Damn. The framed poster board was *big*.

Fortunately, the light rail station at Capitol Hill was only a few blocks away. Still, glass was surprisingly heavy, and while I'd chosen a blue acrylic frame of only moderate weight, I'd insisted on double mattes, so my arms were quivering by the time I reached the platform underground.

Framing Brigham's last protest poster had cost more than I'd have liked, in every way that mattered. "Injustice anywhere is a threat to justice everywhere."

"Do you think it's too trite?" Brigham had asked.

"That's not trite."

"Cliché?"

"It's not cliché, either."

He'd huffed in frustration. "You know what I mean. Everyone says it all the time."

I shook my head. "It's not said nearly enough."

I'd grabbed the sign from the street as Brigham was being loaded into an ambulance, clutching it like a life preserver. It had been leaning against my easy chair ever since. The white poster board was creased. Some of the black marker had run when it landed in a puddle of something on the ground. There was dirt in places.

And a single smudge of blood.

I wasn't even sure it was Brigham's.

"You OK?" a white man in his thirties asked me. "You're shaking."

"Just a 98-pound weakling. Times 2.3." Or thereabout.

"You need me to call anyone?"

I should be finding this sweet, I thought. But mostly, I felt mortified.

"Nope," I said. "I just need to exercise more."

The man shook his head. "You should really try to be more creative," he chided.

"Excuse me?"

"The least you could do is make up a fun story," he said. "'I was a perfectly healthy man until one day I went home with this cute guy, and when he took off his pants, his dick was the size of a gourd. I've trembled ever since.'"

What the—?

The man reached over and put his fingers under my chin. With my mask on, he couldn't see that my jaw had dropped, but it must have been obvious.

"I'm heading the other way," he continued, "to UW. But here's my number." He handed me a business card.

"For a Good Time," I read, "Call…"

"It's so much easier buying a box of these than scribbling above the toilet paper dispenser in every bathroom stall."

He nodded a "See you later" and moved to the northbound side of the platform.

Old and frail, then, was apparently my successful marketing strategy.

But a business card wasn't a bad idea. I could even include my phone number in Braille.

The Angle Lake train pulled into the station, and I climbed aboard, sitting in the disability section. I forced myself to focus on the business card so I wouldn't look back over my shoulder to the platform and check if the young man was watching me. Three white "raindrops" had been placed strategically around the lettering. Once we left the station, I pulled out my phone and entered Burton's number in my Contacts.

Then I wondered if he was an escort.

If I had the money, I'd be fine with that. Still, it'd be nice to cook meals together with someone again.

My mission president in Rome had told us that our two years partnered with assigned companions would prepare us for marriage, but the elder in charge of cooking each week had always cooked alone.

***

Passing through the Pioneer Square station as we approached the end of the downtown tunnel, I could see all four escalators blocked off with yellow tape and orange plastic barriers. Not a single transit security guard was in sight. Several four-by-eight frames made to hold advertising were empty. Two lights were out and three others flickered as if ready to join their ranks.

I'd debated for months now where to hang the framed poster board. I felt closest to Brigham in the bedroom, but hanging it there ensured I'd never be intimate with another man again. Putting it in the living room would cast a pall over any socializing, too.

It would get too humid in the bathroom. And that didn't leave many other options. So I'd covered one of the small windows in the kitchen nook and nailed a picture hook into the wall just above it, waiting for the protest sign.

Like the Madonna boxes we used to make fun of in Napoli.

At Mount Baker, a man with a long Native braid boarded, reminding me it was almost time for my monthly donation to Real Rent. I could never commit to an automatic monthly charge, but I did write reminders on the dinosaur calendar hanging beside my desk.

The first Friday every month, I sent a $10 payment to Justice Democrats. The next Friday, Our Revolution received a few dollars. Greenpeace got money the following Friday and Real Rent the last.

If a month had a fifth Friday, I contributed to documentaries or other film projects on crowdfunding sites. It wasn't much, and there were dozens of other causes just as important, so I usually felt frustrated rather than useful.

And I'd just spent far more framing Brigham's last protest poster than I set aside for an entire month's worth of donations. It was a selfish extravagance.

We passed a Teen Center on MLK, carved Chinese lions near Columbia City, a jewelry repair shop, and a Vietnamese restaurant.

I watched as two officers talked to a black man in front of a Driver Education office and gripped my framed poster board so tightly my fingers looked whiter than ever.

***

"Oh, for fuck's sake!" I muttered when the forty-something white woman marched onto the train. She was pulling her suitcase, apparently heading for the airport, but she surely didn't expect to board.

Her T-shirt read, "COVID vaccinations are the Mark of the Beast!"

She was going to the airport just to make a scene.

I'd been in high school when barcodes were introduced on products. A Baptist friend of mine told me her pastor warned everyone not to buy anything with one on it, that it was the Mark of the Beast. I heard another friend claim that credit cards were the Mark.

My own parents warned me never to buy a book published by Doubleday because the company's address was 666 Fifth Avenue.

Last night, a reporter for a major right-wing network claimed the vaccine contained a bioluminescent marker called luciferase to track people.

The woman with the Satanic T-shirt was humming what sounded like a hymn. I thought about encouraging her to find a better way to take a moral stand but decided to let the airline staff deal with it.

I wondered what Kevin would think of me.

I knew what Kevin would think.

***

The cute Latino was on the train, but so were scores of other riders. Standing room only, and I wasn't close enough to stand next to the guy. I could see him texting, still awake, and planned what I might say as I exited. "Llámame." "Envíame un mensaje." I'd have to leave immediately after handing him my number, though, because if he responded, I wouldn't be able to understand any possibly relevant comments. At least with text, I had a fighting chance.

A white man boarded at SODO wearing a T-shirt showing two assault rifles. It complemented the light blue surgical mask he wore…on his forehead. A young Asian woman boarded with a cup of coffee, which she spilled the moment we took off.

"The train will be stopping momentarily for an operator change," a recorded message played. "The train will be moving shortly. We thank you for your patience."

We stopped on the elevated section by the train yard filled with a few trains and room for dozens more. I could make out Mount Rainier in the distance. Another hot, clear day. Then we were on our way again.

My phone pinged and I pulled it out of my bag. I almost hoped it was Burton. We'd had a fun time last night, though that "gourd" comment had been false advertising. I'd threatened to sue. And then he'd playfully tied me up and inserted a dildo reminding me of my favorite Carlo Masi film.

The experience had been a bit like popping a pimple. "Let the healing begin," I'd told myself as I left his apartment.

Intimacy.

Physical, though, not emotional. And Burton had made it clear he was a one-and-done kind of guy.

"Went to see 2 properties in Langley." It was Jeremy up in Surrey. "Too many anti-vaxxers. Agent planning surgery and only wants blood from unvaxxed donors."

We entered the tunnel under Beacon Hill, and I glanced over at the Latino guy. Still awake. A good sign. I wondered if he lived anywhere near Harrison in Tukwila. We'd met in the video store in White Center before the pandemic when I was buying a double penetration dildo for Brigham's birthday, an activity I'd introduced into the relationship. Brigham and I were both versatile, though he leaned top and I leaned bottom. Most of the time when we wanted double penetration, it consisted of one real dick and a rubber one working in tandem.

I'd fucked Harrison a couple of times at his place, with just my one dick, but then there was the pandemic. And the protests. And disaster.

When things finally started looking like they might be lightening up, I'd ventured a text his way.

"No vaccine," he'd texted back. "No mask for me."

We'd never talked politics, so I'd had no idea he was a nut. I'd texted back, "OK. I'll text again when things calm down." But I knew I'd never be texting him.

Odd you could miss someone's asshole when that was almost all you really knew about the guy.

I sure hoped the Latino wasn't a nutcase, too. The black man running against the governor of California in the recall election wanted reparations…for slaveowners. Some folks in South Carolina had hosted a Get COVID party to encourage folks to generate "natural immunity." A televangelist was calling out his congregation for not donating more money, saying God wanted him to have a bigger private jet right *now*.

Nearer My God...

Once out on MLK, the light rail passed a dialysis center, a chiropractic clinic, and a dental office. We passed a mosque housed in a storefront, an elaborate Buddhist temple, and a run-of-the-mill church.

The Latino guy was nodding off. Porca la miseria. But no, he was awake again. I wondered if I should get off a couple of stops early and slip him my number while I had a chance.

And now he was nodding off once more. OK, I'd get off at Othello and catch the next train home. I stood and made my way to the landing in front of the doors, inching closer and closer to the disability bench. I pulled the slip of paper out of my wallet with my name and phone number.

Another passenger preparing to get off jostled me, and I bumped into the cute man's white cane, hooked to the rail, knocking it to the floor.

"Scusa!" I said. It came out in Italian, since apparently I only had room in my head for two languages—English and "everything else."

Dammit! And I'd even prepared for an emergency like this.

The doors opened and I rushed off the train, hoping he couldn't see me clearly enough to peg me as the clumsy jerk next time I saw him on the platform.

Chapter Eight: The Road to Enlightenment

I tapped my Orca card against the reader and nodded at the heavy black driver. He rolled his eyes and turned away.

Straight men were convinced every gay man was after them. I wouldn't have turned the guy away, but he wasn't high on my list of fantasies. I hoped he wasn't reacting this way because I was giving off desperate vibes.

It was even worse when gay men gave that "put upon" look for having to bear the terrible burden of being noticed by another gay man.

I'd rather be alone than needy. Even when I was exceptionally horny and browsed hookup sites, once I beat off, all I could think was, "Boy, that was a whole lot simpler than getting involved with another human." And far less time consuming. I'd have the rest of the evening free to watch *Captain Marleau.*

Yoo yoo!

And my goodness, the things people demanded in those ads. "Come sit in my rim chair." "Smell my feet and lick the cheese from between my toes." "Leave your door unlocked, lean over your sofa when I come in, and don't take off your blindfold."

Did anyone ever answer these ads?

Consenting adults could do whatever they wanted, I supposed. There was someone for everyone.

Brigham and I had always known we weren't soulmates. Neither of us believed in such a thing. But there was a lot to be said for liking the person you loved.

I wanted to encourage the heavyset driver to "Rest well and dream of large women," but instead I headed down the aisle to find a seat.

It wasn't difficult. Only two other riders were on board.

Not like the buses in Napoli. Once, at the end of a long day of proselytizing, my companion and I waited to head back to our neighborhood up near Vomero. When the bus finally arrived, it was so crowded people were already hanging out the doors. My companion forced his way on but I couldn't manage it.

"Ci vediamo a casa, Anziano," I'd said. It was a terrible sin to be separated.

Suddenly, a woman, probably in her late twenties, reached down out of the bus and grabbed my tie. She pulled me aboard to take her place and stepped off to wait for the next bus.

I remembered realizing that she'd just performed more genuine service that day than the missionary she'd helped.

***

"Got any advice?" I asked. Tommy was an odd mix of savvy and clueless. Maybe I'd luck out.

"If you want to hook up with a Hispanic dude," Tommy said, "you need to know the word 'polla.'"

"Chicken?" I asked.

Tommy shook his head. "Polla means cock." Loud, but thank God we were still at the bus stop.

If I hadn't even bothered to look up how to ask the Latino on the train if he wanted to have coffee with me, was I really committed enough to see this through?

"Puedo chuparte la polla?" Tommy said. "That's all you need to know. You can figure the rest out with your hands." He laughed. "Or your throat."

I nodded. "Thanks. I appreciate it."

"Prove it." He grabbed his belt and pulled his pants away from his abdomen like someone talking while wearing a mask. I glanced around. Cars passed in both directions, of course, but no one was on the sidewalk. I dipped my hand past the belt.

"You go commando," I said.

"Don't you?" Tommy asked. "You should. Everyone should."

His cock was semi-hard and growing harder. I sighed the way I had when Brigham surprised me with cheesecake, back when I could eat it. "Not bad." I rubbed my finger lightly over the tip of his penis and felt something wet.

Had I stimulated him enough to instigate pre-cum that quickly? Or…

"Here comes the bus," I said, withdrawing my hand and wiping my finger on my pants. I carried a small bottle of hand sanitizer in my bag, but I'd wait until after Tommy transferred to the light rail before using it. I was already pretty good about not touching my face while commuting, so I should be OK until then.

Tommy boarded ahead of me. While I was tapping my Orca card, he turned back and said, loudly, "You could have licked your finger, you know. I don't have any STDs."

***

A middle-aged Indian couple boarded the 11 with a young man and a young woman, both in their twenties. The young man was taller than the others and much heavier, with hunched shoulders, his face tilted downward but his eyes searching the rest of us. He jerked his arm and clenched his fists, freezing in the middle of the aisle, but the older woman beckoned him forward while the younger woman said something to him softly and guided him along.

The parents sat together on one side of the aisle while their son and daughter sat on the other side.

We rode for almost fifteen minutes together. They didn't get off the bus until we reached the Paramount. Looked like Randy Rainbow was coming to Seattle. I'd seen the family deboard here on previous occasions. They probably lived somewhere downtown.

The parents never expressed any frustration with their son, who I took to be autistic but of course couldn't really know. More impressive was the daughter, who also never expressed any frustration, never acted like her brother's behavior was a burden or annoyance.

Just a nice family outing together, maybe to the Japanese Garden or Arboretum.

Perhaps public transportation wasn't the time suck for others that it was for me, if they could travel with people they loved.

***

"Whew!" The young black man shook his head. "I'm high. Got some Bombay a little while ago."

I nodded politely, though I had no idea what he was talking about. He'd been rambling since I boarded the bus.

People joked about "dog years" or "gay years," but neither compared to "bus minutes." Five of those were the equivalent of forty-five non-bus minutes.

"I fell asleep and stayed on too long and now I'm heading back the other way." He tapped the seat in front of him to accompany the music in his head. "I lost my phone so I bet my girlfriend is mad."

I stared at the Stop Requested sign for deliverance.

A few moments later, a thin white man in his thirties boarded. Perhaps if he sat close enough, the talker's attention might be diverted. As the new rider slowly advanced, though, I saw his mask bearing a huge "Q" against a blue background.

I'd just read a baffling report that 21% of Mormons believed Q conspiracies.

I didn't want him to sit near us.

More disconcerting were the polls showing that 30% of Republicans supported violence to "save" the country. For viewers of far-right media, the number was 40%.

That worked out to around thirteen million Americans.

And it didn't even require "violence" for these folks to do damage.

People were gargling with iodine rather than getting vaccinated. Some claimed that nurses recounting the horrors of dying patients were crisis actors.

The black man across the aisle droned on. I nodded every few moments, trying to tune him out. I focused instead on a black woman applying hair milk styling foam to her hair. Over and over and over again.

The bus seconds ticked by.

The man laughed at something he said and I nodded once more.

Sometimes, just sitting could be exhausting.

***

When the customer had spit into the carrot bin, Gail had pulled out her phone.

"Don't call the police," I said as calmly as possible.

"But he could be spreading COVID!" she whispered loudly. "He could be spreading hepatitis and AIDS!"

I trudged up the stairs now to the Mount Baker platform. I'd avoided taking the 11 downtown to Westlake after work because of the game. Hundreds of folks would be on light rail heading to Stadium station, a nightmare even before the pandemic. Instead, I'd caught an 8 to the transit center and then crossed Rainier to the light rail station.

But the escalators here rarely worked, and the last time I'd tried the elevator, there was human feces on the floor. A political statement, probably, rather than an issue of privacy, as there was plenty of privacy behind the entire back wall of the station, which bordered a chained off parking lot that was always empty.

I had to pause ten steps from the top to catch my breath. A young black man passed on my left. Once on the platform, I saw several other folks waiting, all but one of them black.

Their expressions were hard, their clothes slightly frayed, and I remembered the night I'd been mugged on Capitol Hill years ago walking home from a bar.

So I headed to the far end of the platform nearest Beacon Hill, keeping track with my peripheral vision to make sure no one was following me.

Across the tracks on the opposite platform, a white woman texted someone on her phone.

At the supermarket today, Gail had actually listened to me, not one of her usual behaviors. With her finger poised over the number screen, I held out my hand, palm down, and lowered it as if deflating a beach ball. "Our produce is already covered with E. coli," I said, "and God only knows what other bacteria. That's why we post signs telling customers to wash it before eating."

"But he's still spitting."

The train emerged from the hill and pulled up to the station. When the doors opened, I found a seat in the main section, across from the disability bench.

"This is the train to Angle Lake."

The doors closed and we took off. Almost home. Only another half hour, God willing. We passed the Filipino Community Center, a huge piece of iron artwork with poetry carved out of it, and a tiny store selling plus-sized women's clothing.

"He's black, Gail," I'd said. "You didn't call the police on the white woman sitting in the middle of the floor and throwing a tantrum because you asked her to mask."

As we pulled out of the Columbia City station a few minutes later, I noticed an elderly Asian man doing push ups against the bike rack.

"This is different!" Gail had hissed at me. "He's—"

"He's black. Don't call the police."

I touched my left cheek as we passed a Used Car lot, still sore from where the spitter had thrown a Honey Crisp apple at me. At least that had seemed to calm whatever was happening inside his head. Gail had pulled out her phone again, I again waved her down, and we both held our breath until the man slowly sauntered out of the store.

I wasn't at all sure that was a victory for anyone.

When we crossed Henderson, I could see the 106 on MLK waiting to turn. I dashed out the doors the second they opened, saw the countdown at the crosswalk sign as I ran toward it—9, 8, 7, 6—and sprinted across the street without checking for traffic.

But I made it, my spleen contracting painfully and a twinge shooting through my right foot, just as the bus pulled up to the shelter.

My cheek throbbed like hemorrhoids contending with a new dildo.

***

A young man, mid-twenties, boarded with another young man and sat across the aisle from me. They may have been a couple but weren't "obviously" gay, despite the shorter man having painted his fingernails gray. The taller of the men was wearing an Iron Maiden T-shirt. He laughed at something his companion had just said.

"Aren't you too young to know who Iron Maiden is?" I asked. It was hard to banter with no facial expressions to assist. And because interrupting a conversation was obnoxious.

"Oh, no!" the man protested. "They're great! I love *The Number of the Beast* and *Killers* and *No Prayer for the Dying*!"

I gave him a thumbs up. He nodded his approval of my approval and resumed chatting with his friend.

But a few seconds later, he turned back to me. "I'm sorry," he said. "I didn't ask what *your* favorite Iron Maiden song was."

"Oh," I said, unprepared for reciprocity, "I like the Carpenters."

Chapter Nine: It's Not the Destination, It's the Journey

Pop! Pop! Pop! Pop!

I didn't recognize the sound until the people around me began running. One of the bullets shattered the bus shelter's back panel. Another struck a car in the parking lot of the bank beyond the fence.

A young black woman with long, blue braids was already crouched behind a garbage can. A heavyset, middle-aged Latina knelt behind a tree.

I dropped to the ground and lay flat.

If you could call an Alfred Hitchcock-shaped mound flat.

Pop! Pop! Pop! Pop! Pop!

How many bullets were there, for God's sake? More than one gun? And who was shooting?

The gunfire stopped as quickly as it had started, replaced by the sound of wheels squealing against the pavement, the pungent smell of burned rubber in the air. I struggled to my knees and then to my feet, patting myself like Tom Arnold in *True Lies*.

No blood, despite hitting the ground so quickly. And no one else seemed hurt, either.

What the hell was that all about?

Had some neo-Nazi casually noticed a gay man waiting for the bus and opened fire? Perhaps a white supremacist was aiming at the other folks. Was that middle-aged Latina in a gang? That young Asian man with a skateboard wearing a starched shirt and crisply pressed jeans?

Were there gay Asian skateboard gangs?

Sheesh, how many clichés could I bundle together?

"Thank you! Thank you!" An Asian woman, maybe thirty, hugged a six-year-old girl to her chest and nodded at me over and over.

She apparently believed I'd deliberately shielded the girl with my body. But it looked to me as if the girl had taken it upon herself to seek shelter behind the largest object in the area.

Several officers had quit the police force in the wake of last year's protests, and a couple more had been dismissed for their participation in or support of the insurrection back in January. But officers still arrived at the scene within minutes.

A few folks stayed to talk, but the rest of us had places to go. I walked down to the next stop and waited for another 7.

***

Tommy dragged me to the back of the bus and pushed me into the corner. "If I can't get laid at the Bear Trap," he said, loudly, "I wanna at least make out on the way home."

Pundits talked about the normalization of fascism and white supremacy. The normalization of inappropriate public displays of affection was a surprisingly slippery slope, too.

Tommy pulled down his mask, with its image of a sledgehammer on front. As he thrust his tongue into my mouth, I wondered if I should get the mask I'd seen online the day before, black fabric with a vivid red virus particle in the middle.

Tommy's tongue tasted like beer.

I'd searched for "gay face masks" online as well, thinking perhaps a Rainbow Flag or bear paw or even a leather pride flag might help me advertise myself at work or while commuting. Perhaps in a gay bar, a mask with an image of an erect penis would help me stand out, if it didn't blend in with the crowd and instead act as camouflage.

Tommy's fingers pinched my left nipple. I put my hand on his chest.

I'd been riding my stationary bike almost every night while binge-watching the Swedish suffragette series, *Miss Friman's War*. I'd also reduced my daily protein bar intake by one.

I thought I was too tired after a long day at work and boring night at the Bear Trap to get an erection, but when Tommy reached for my crotch, I discovered I was mistaken. That reminded me I'd brought something along for just this scenario, an old bath towel I pulled out of my bag and flung over us now to act as a body mask. We were breathing a bit heavily, after all.

Just as importantly, it made me feel slightly less perverted when I grabbed Tommy's crotch in return.

Lots of self-delusion to go around.

***

"I don't believe in masks," the woman said emphatically, "and I don't believe in this rushed vaccine." She was white, in her fifties, and wearing a button-down shirt fashioned from what looked like an actual U.S. flag.

The white woman she was traveling with, perhaps a few years older, wore a T-shirt that warned all around her not to tread on Texas.

Not all tourists were assholes. I just couldn't help noticing the ones who were.

"I don't want anyone shoving something down my throat," the friend informed me.

It would have been pointless to remind them about breathing tubes, so instead, I shrugged. "Are you sure? Because I can deep throat, and it's usually pretty fun."

It was a lot easier to recognize a look of horror when a person's face was completely uncovered.

At least they stayed more than six feet away from me the rest of the trip.

***

Walking down the aisle, I spotted a white woman in her late twenties wearing a tube top barely covering her nipples. She swayed in her seat, so drunk I tried estimating a safe perimeter from any projectile lunch sharing that might occur before I had a chance to deboard.

***

Sheldon on *Big Bang* had his "bus pants." I decided to come up with some "bus shirts."

The idea didn't spring from the deep throat incident on the train but from seeing a woman who boarded the 48 one morning wearing a T-shirt that read, "Jesus loves me…doggy style."

If a man had been wearing such a shirt, I might have worked up the nerve to give my number to him. Perhaps not, but it wouldn't have felt inappropriately inappropriate. I considered buying a similar shirt for myself to help with advertising but was afraid anything that sexual might get me arrested for indecency or simply beaten up for being gay.

As if groping Tommy wasn't enough.

Still, something off-putting could be useful. I was wearing my first physical distancing T-shirt today, one I'd had printed reading "Talk to me about the god Weripus." The name was completely made up. I hoped it sounded odd enough to make people leery.

Aboard the bus, though, no one got close enough to read the invitation. Then an unexpected problem occurred when someone did read it at my first transfer point.

"Who's Weripus?" a young black woman asked. She had a backpack slung over her shoulder, perhaps a student on her way to UW.

"He's the god of kittens and snakes," I said. The woman was wearing a mask, and her tone seemed genuine, so there was no reason to alienate her. I just wasn't willing to lose on my first attempt.

The woman's brows furrowed. "I'm not familiar with that mythology."

"*Mythology*?"

"Oh, I'm sorry, I meant—"

"Weripus will not be pleased."

The woman froze, her eyes locked on mine.

I didn't know what to do from here. "Do you have any kittens or snakes?" I asked.

The woman stared a moment longer and then burst into laughter. "Oh my God!" she said, wiping her eyes. "You really had me going for a minute. I want one of those shirts, too!"

***

Most bus riders understood the importance of "the spot." Each stop had a certain zone where the front doors opened 95% of the time. There was a range, of course, and by its very nature, the spot wasn't fixed.

Sometimes, it was right next to the sign. Other times, it was in front of the bus shelter or bench. Still other times, there was no obvious reasoning behind it. But each spot was consistent.

If I was the first to arrive at a bus stop, I immediately positioned myself in the right spot. It helped the driver when passengers could begin boarding quickly, which also helped anyone else who'd arrived after me. Sometimes, an elderly person or someone with lots of bags showed up after I'd claimed the spot, and though I'd keep control of it until the bus pulled up, I'd usually step aside at that point and wave the other person on ahead.

Other times, the driver sized up the situation as she approached and deliberately stopped a few feet short of the spot or instead overshot it, in order to open the doors in front of the other rider.

But there were other times, probably once or twice a week, when I was the only person at the bus stop, and I was standing in the exact spot where almost every driver opened their doors, yet *this* driver would look at me through the windshield, slow the bus down, and then either stop three feet early *or* keep looking at me as he kept rolling three feet past me. Just as often, they'd do this without locking eyes.

Either way, it felt deliberate.

It probably wasn't. I tuned out as often as possible, too. The driver could have been distracted by a hundred different things, worrying about a suspicious mole on their partner's back, their kid suddenly no longer joking around anymore, pretty much anything.

But it *felt* like a microaggression.

Was the driver doing this because I was white? Because I was a man? Just because they were sick of riders in general that day?

Part of me understood that being the recipient of one or two microaggressions a week was getting off light. Many of the riders I saw every day faced this type of behavior in virtually every aspect of their lives. If just a couple of microaggressions was this wearing on me, I couldn't imagine how a heavier onslaught affected them.

So I made a point of cheerfully greeting the driver after each of these incidents, without any sarcasm. If they needed to get out a little frustration, for whatever reason, I could take it. And if I could improve the bad day they were having even a tiny bit, it was worth a smile.

Hardly a sacrifice worthy of a Nobel Peace Prize, after all.

***

I overshot the Grocery Outlet in Skyway by two stops to force myself to get in a little extra walk. As I was passing the gas station on my way back up the hill, I heard two crows cursing out another bird. It looked like a hawk of some kind. I kept climbing and watched as the hawk broke free of the crows and dove to the pavement.

Cazzo! What a wingspan. The raptor turned, and I saw that its head was covered in white feathers. A goddamned bald eagle.

A car approached, but the eagle didn't budge, scooping up some kind of roadkill while giving the driver what seemed to me an imperious glare. The car stopped. Then a car approaching from the other direction stopped. The eagle finished grabbing what it could and flew away.

I loved living in the Pacific Northwest.

***

An old white man boarded the 48 with his right arm extended in front of him, pointing and wagging his index finger.

There were plenty of mentally ill people on public transportation. Activists were demanding that police officers receive better training on mental health issues, that some emergency calls be directed to mental health experts rather than to people trained to use guns.

But I wondered if the rest of us didn't need some of that mental health training, too. Just like a test was required for citizenship, certain psychological instruction for public transit riders could help us all better understand how to interact, or not interact, with other riders.

I didn't expect that curriculum any time soon, of course. I wasn't *that* crazy.

We passed the Woodcraft Center and an African American museum.

Four police cars were parked behind the Starbucks. The corner of Jackson was still the most desolate part of the Central District, even with several new, seven-story condos. Officers had taped off a large section of the parking lot in front of the auto supply store and an Asian eatery next to it. I could see windows shot out of two cars and a couple dozen evidence markers on the ground, probably where shell casings had landed.

No ambulances, though, and no body bags, thank God.

Everyone knew we could die at any moment. Even young, apparently healthy people died of heart attacks. Anyone could have an aneurysm. And we all knew we could be hit by a bus, or have a plane crash into our house, or find ourselves in a major earthquake or tsunami. A neo-Nazi or other terrorist could blow us up.

But those threats, while real, could feel remote and theoretical. Yet when you reached the age of sixty, fat, with diabetes, the problem wasn't so much that the threat didn't become more believable. It was that the timeline was still vague. I *could* be dead within two years. Or I could linger on in declining health for another twenty.

I traced a finger along my new, bright blue compression sleeves. They really did help me stop picking at my skin.

The purple ones went better with most of my clothes, and I'd bought one pair that was tan but covered with tattoos.

Growing so daring in my old age.

***

"When are you due?" The young black man pointed at my belly and laughed. His two teen friends laughed with him. Clearly, the four pounds I'd lost since I'd started riding my stationary bike were noticeable to no one but me. The bus stop on the corner of Henderson and Rainier could always be a bit tricky. A couple of years earlier, a man who might have been Filipino walked up to me without a word and punched me in the nose.

"Oh, I've got another month left," I told the teenager. "The treatments really slow things down."

The teens turned to one another with sharp, quick movements. "Da fuck?" one of them said.

"My wife doesn't like to go to the birthing classes with me," I continued. "And I could really use some support. You guys interested?" I started the stereotypical Lamaze panting through my mask. "You'll have to learn how to breathe." I paused. "It's *fun.*"

They looked at one another again and quickly walked away down the street.

Cool guys didn't run.

The most embarrassing part of the entire encounter was realizing I was the bigger jerk.

Chapter Ten: Take the Long Way Home

Going to the Bear Trap on a night Tommy wasn't there wasn't any more rewarding. While I might feel uncomfortable around him, he'd only ever been nice to me. I made my way toward the bus stop, realizing I'd become one of the trolls I'd dreaded so much my first years after coming out.

"I'm not a Boy Scout any longer," someone said, touching my elbow, "but can I help you cross the street?"

I turned to see a white man in his late thirties. I'd apparently been so lost in thought I was just standing on the corner looking dazed. The guy was masked, trim without being thin, and exuded sexual energy I could almost taste.

"Um, uh, sure," I said.

"Where you going?"

My mind finally started waking up. "Your bedroom?"

The man laughed. "You want a *really* good deed!"

I shrugged. "I used to be a Boy Scout, too," I said. "So I'm prepared." I tapped my bag. "Lube, condoms, and I douched before leaving work."

The man nodded in an exaggerated fashion. After so many months in masks, many of us were probably ready to start watching old silent movies again. My favorite had been *The Unholy Three.*

I wasn't *that* old, of course, but silents aired late on Friday evenings when I was a kid, and I used to listen to reruns of *The Shadow* Saturday afternoons on the radio.

I was out of touch, even then.

I also used to buy twelve-minute reels of scenes from full-length movies. *The Poseidon Adventure* in black and white, with no sound. Twelve black and white, silent minutes of *Planet of the Apes.*

God, I *was* old. The other day, I almost yelled at someone to get off my lawn.

"I never made Eagle," the young man beside me said, his hand still on my elbow, "but this sounds like a project I can complete."

"Twice?" I asked. He was young enough, after all.

"My name's Anthony."

"Todd."

"I'm a Logger driver, but I'm on foot tonight. If you're coming home with me, it's just a short bus ride from here."

Almost no one liked driving on Capitol Hill.

I wished that had been true last summer.

"Will you need help getting undressed?" Anthony asked.

"You'll have trouble keeping my clothes on before we make it to your place."

***

The smoke was a little worse today, the Air Quality Index at 80. Nowhere near as bad as it had been last year, when we topped 300, or even last week when we registered 104.

Wildfires were ravaging parts of Turkey and Algeria. Forty million acres had burned in Siberia. Greenville, California had been destroyed by flames. All state parks in California were now closed to the public.

I decided to walk down to Tommy's bus stop this morning, feeling bad for avoiding him lately. He ground his crotch into mine as we hugged. The pressure felt so good it was hard to pull away.

"You always get me horny before work," he complained with a grunt. He pulled his mask down to kiss me, but before he could approach again, he sniffled heavily. It was probably just allergies, perhaps the smoke, but I took a step back.

"You get me horny, too," I said.

Tommy shook his head like a wet dog trying to dry off, exhaling like a horse. "Smmyphh!" I thought at first it was an expression of sexual frustration, but then I realized it was his way of shaking the mucus out of his nostrils. Afterward, he wiped his nose with his fingertips. I took another step back.

We waited for the bus almost ten minutes, and Tommy kept blowing snot out of his nose as we chatted. “The Proud Boys threw fireworks into the back of a gay bar in White Center,” he said. “Smmyphh!”

I’d seen no reports identifying who’d thrown the fireworks, just a few doors down from last month’s arson.

“Those motherfuckers.” Tommy whinnied again and then wiped the tip of his nose once more with his fingers.

“All they want to do is keep their wives at home and beat them at the end of the day.”

Smmyphh!

I looked up the street for the bus, but it was nowhere in sight.

“And they beat their kids, too.” He wiped his nose again with his fingers. I stood a full six feet away. “When I was thirteen, I went home with a friend, and his father came home drunk and beat us both.” He exhaled loudly before wiping his nose yet again.

Why hadn’t I waited at my own stop?

“See this scar near my eye?”

Smmyphh!

“Here comes the 106.”

He turned to look.

“Oh!” I said. “I forgot something at home! Damn! I’ll have to catch the next bus. You have a good day, Tommy.” I waved and started heading back up the hill.

When I boarded the next bus fifteen minutes later, the first thing I noticed was a young black man wearing a baseball cap that read, "Be nice."

***

Earbud day.

I chose my "calm" playlist.

An airline passenger flying out of Atlanta had tried to bite the ear off a flight attendant yesterday. The FBI had caught an incel in Ohio who was planning to kill 3000 women. And two homeless men here in Seattle had been arrested for throwing rocks off an overpass through the windshields of cars driving on the freeway below.

Lauren Daigle sang "You Say" so beautifully I didn't even mind it was a religious song.

Meghan Trainor and John Legend promised to love their significant others, "Like I'm Gonna Lose You."

Christina Perri softly cooed, "A Thousand Years," the theme song from the *Twilight* series, written by a BYU grad and set near the Washington rain forest.

Imagine Dragons committed to full devotion in "Follow You." The frontman was a straight Mormon ally, and the cute music video for the song featured one of the actors from *Latter Days*.

Listening to Paramore sing "The Only Exception," I realized once more I was never going to see Brigham again.

***

A white man, about fifty, entered from the right and then stood by the doors on the left side of the train. He was wearing a light gray sweatshirt with the name of a prominent School of Public Health.

He wasn't wearing a mask.

***

It was years after buses and light rail implemented audio announcements of upcoming stops and Next Stop display signs that listed approaching street names before I realized those weren't just frills to make public transportation "nicer." They were essential for people with disabilities.

Southbound light rail announced, "This is the train to Angle Lake," and the northbound line announced, "This is the train to the University of Washington," at every single stop.

Brigham, who'd only ridden public transit on his way to or from a protest, complained one day that the repetition was annoying.

"Do you remember the *I Love Lucy* episode," I'd asked, "where Lucy gets a loving cup stuck on her head?"

My favorite episode was Lucy setting her nose on fire. Brigham's had always been the train robbery. Both of us liked the Freddie Fillmore quiz show episodes. We watched reruns together on Sunday mornings, if I had the day off.

"And when she gets disoriented," I'd continued, "she asks a man on the platform where she is."

Brigham had chuckled. "And the guy says, 'You're on *Earth*!'"

I'd set out the DVD with the train robbery episode two months ago but hadn't worked up the nerve to slide it into the player yet.

"As annoying as it is to hear that Angle Lake announcement ten times every day," I'd told Brigham, "it's even more annoying for a visually impaired person to get on the wrong train and not be able to figure it out for another fifteen minutes."

The conversation had shifted then to the latest stories in the news, an officer shooting a European journalist in the eye with a rubber bullet, and a black woman chaining herself to a Confederate statue until it was brought down.

As we'd stepped off the train in Rainier Beach, Brigham had squeezed my hand. "Thank you," he said. "That announcement still sounds exactly the same. But it's not the least bit annoying anymore."

***

"Yeah, suck it, baby!"

I'd taken a History of the English Language course in college, but vocabulary always seemed to come down to the basics.

"Suck that cock, cocksucker! Choke on my dick!"

The words to Viola Valentino's "Romantici" floated through my brain.

It was 3:30 in the morning. Anthony hadn't even called when he finished his drives for Logger, had just started ringing my doorbell until I answered, and had then wanted to drive me around the block while I sucked his dick. Since the alternative was to go back to bed regretting the missed opportunity, I took him up on the offer.

"You don't mind the camera, do you?"

I glanced up from Anthony's lap to see him pointing at a tiny device just over the driver's side door. The video was mostly going to show the back of my head in a darkened car, and it wasn't as if I was running for city council, so what did I care?

Of course, he probably should have asked permission *before* the filming began.

I kept plugging away—he was taking an exceptionally long time, but then he'd had a long day, too—so I didn't notice at first that he'd stopped driving.

"I'm gonna cum!"

I renewed my efforts, not wanting to let the chance to finally finish slip away, but he pulled my head off his lap just in time for me to watch him spurt, the geyser just missing my nose.

"Ahh!" he breathed. "I love getting that cum shot on camera."

Once he finished shooting, I wasn't sure what to do next. Was it my turn now? Would he simply drive me home with his pants unzipped and my own dick still hoping to pop?

"Clean me up?" he asked.

When he made no motion toward a washcloth or tissue, I finally understood what he wanted and did as he'd asked.

"Thanks," he said after I licked up the last drop embedded in his pubic hair. "Can you walk from here?"

I looked out the window. We were parked behind an RV along the stretch of road by a boarded up Native American drug and alcohol treatment facility, probably ten blocks from my house.

"Sure," I said.

I climbed out of the car. Anthony gave me a quick salute with two fingers and drove off. Ten blocks at 4:00 in the morning. I could probably call a Logger, but…

I heard a familiar hum and turned. A 107 was coming! At this time of night, if a bus route was in operation at all, there was only one bus an hour. I ran to the bus stop, waving like a madman.

When the doors opened, the driver shouted at me. "Put on a mask!"

"Sorry," I muttered. I didn't have my Orca card, either. Or my wallet. I could only imagine what the driver was thinking. But he let me board.

White privilege had its privileges.

"I'll just grab one of these," I said, pointing to the dispenser.

"And wipe that...stuff off your chin."

He could probably smell more than see it. I'd been rooting around in Anthony's crotch rather thoroughly.

After a few years on the job, bus drivers probably experienced far too many things they never wanted to share with their loved ones. I didn't know if I should be impressed by that or just deeply, deeply sad.

***

I decided to give the "bus shirt" idea another try. I'd considered weaponizing body odor by no longer wearing antiperspirant, but I did have to smell myself, too.

Stepping off the 106, I dodged around a tree, swerved to avoid the black guy shouting into the air near the ATM, and crossed over to Bay 2. A short Asian man, masked, hovered near the trash can reading what looked like a Chinese newspaper. Korean print was a little different, Thai quite different, and Vietnamese hardly looked Asian at all. But without little clues like that, I often couldn't distinguish one group of Asians from another. Part of me felt that the distinctions were artificial anyway, but another part felt that not noticing was dismissive.

Yet white guilt also felt unhelpful, so I just tried to pay better attention.

Two young black women wearing hijabs, fully masked, chatted next to the bus stop sign. A black man of indeterminate age slept huddled on one of the bus shelter benches, a pool of urine beneath him.

"My therapist says I should talk more with strangers." It was the equivalent of walking into a gay bar and announcing, "I'm lonely!" The shirt cost more than I would have liked, but social distancing on public transit was therapeutic, and therapy wasn't free.

The 48 pulled up a few minutes later and I debated boarding but decided I wasn't up for the longer walk to work. I'd skip another protein bar.

"I've been told I'm a good listener."

"Excuse me?"

An elderly black woman pointed at my shirt. Her mask was made from a flower print. Daisies.

"Oh, I…"

"You need a listening ear?" she asked. "Want some advice?" She reached out as if to grasp my arm but pulled back. "What can I do to help?"

I stood there unable to speak, embarrassed to have taken advantage of the woman.

"You *do* want to talk, don't you?" She shook her head and then chuckled. "I've heard it all. Six kids and fourteen grandchildren." More qualified to listen than a bus driver.

"Oh, my."

"Do you talk to *your* kids?" she asked. When I shook my head, she nodded in return. "I know how it is."

We then talked about her family for the next ten minutes. And it did seem to help. When the 8 came, I motioned for her to board first, but she waved me off. "I just got off the 14," she said. "I'm heading to the grocery." She pointed up the street. "You have a blessed day."

***

Since the libraries were still closed and I had no printer of my own, I'd gone to Georgetown to print one of Brigham's poems to send to Makenna. The bus stop to get back was across from the old city hall, now a dental office, and just half a block from Boeing Field. Planes flew so low that the two-story dental office had installed a flashing red light on top of the roof to help planes make it past.

The trash can here was always overflowing. Aluminum cans, paper cups, and food wrappers littered the sidewalk around the garbage can, on either side and behind the bus shelter, and on the bus shelter bench as well. A sign declaring "We Buy Houses for Cash!" was stapled to a light post. Just below that was a homemade "Missing" poster featuring the photo of a young woman, possibly indigenous.

Standing a few feet away was a white man with a deep tan suggesting either outdoor labor or homelessness. The muscles had me leaning more toward the first possibility, but his pink sweatshirt with the words "Spread the Love" led more toward the second. A man drinking a beer stood a few feet past him, and I heard the man in the pink sweatshirt casually mention that he was in recovery. The other man didn't pursue the conversation, and the first guy let it drop.

Just then, an Access van pulled up to the shelter, and the driver stepped out. An elderly white woman across the street began yelling. "I can't walk! I need you on *this* side! Why are you so stupid?"

The driver threw up his hands. We were on a one-way street.

The man in the pink sweatshirt crossed to the sidewalk in front of the dental office and offered his arm, slowly escorting the woman across the street, holding out his free arm to block traffic as she took tiny, shuffling steps.

When they finally arrived at the van, the woman began yelling again. "I've been waiting two hours!"

The driver closed his eyes and took a deep breath, but the man in the pink sweatshirt stopped the tirade with a pleasant smile. Neither he nor the elderly woman were wearing masks. "The important thing is he's here now," he said. "Let's get you on board."

The man in the sweatshirt helped her in and then came to stand next to me as the van took off. We waited another fifteen minutes for our bus in silence.

Chapter Eleven: Strangers on a Bus

It was going to be a waste of time. I knew it. If the weight reduction clinic refused to list their prices online, refused even to discuss pricing over the phone, whatever the price might be, it was out of my range.

But I had to give it a shot.

I caught the 106 to Renton. At the end of the line, I strolled about, looking for the bus to Bellevue. The transit center consisted of two streets forming a T, and there were too many possibilities to figure out the right bus stop immediately. I stood at the sign advertising the 560 for three minutes before I realized it was the sign for the 560 coming *back* from Bellevue.

I looked across the street and saw the 560 already at another bay, ready to leave. I dashed across the street and reached the doors just as the driver closed them. He opened for me, I climbed on and found a seat, and the bus took off.

These Sound Transit buses were *nice*, the seats comfy, with high backs allowing riders to relax in their own personal space. We made a couple more stops in town and then pulled onto the freeway, zooming north in the morning sun. But I'd taken a seat on the wrong side of the bus. Even with the air conditioner, the sun beat through the glass mercilessly. I'd pay more attention on the way back.

Liposuction would probably be the cheaper of the options I was considering today, but it would mean leaving behind too much loose skin. Cool sculpting would cost more but shrink the skin as the procedure advanced. My biggest concern was how much fat could be removed at a time, something else their website refused to specify. If it was only four or five pounds, that would mean fifteen separate procedures. Even at a thousand dollars apiece, that would be thousands out of my range.

Naturally, weight reduction wasn't covered under my health insurance. Neither was dental or vision. It probably didn't cover hearing, either, though that wasn't a problem yet, so I hadn't checked.

We made stops along freeway ramps in a couple of communities and arrived in Bellevue in a little over twenty minutes. It had taken less time to get from Seattle to Renton to Bellevue than it took to go from south Seattle to central Seattle for work.

Porca la misera.

I pulled out my notes. Another ten-minute walk and I should be there.

But as I passed Neiman Marcus and Prada and Chanel and Gucci, I realized that even if the procedure could remove eighty pounds of fat in one sitting, there must be a reason the clinic was in this neighborhood.

***

People used the word "know" when what they really meant was "suspect very strongly."

But now I did know. I not only couldn't afford weight reduction procedures but I wasn't even qualified for them. "Your fat is all in your stomach," the young white woman who evaluated me said, without lifting my shirt, weighing me, or examining me at all. She'd simply read my answers to the questionnaire which I'd been asked to fill out in the lobby.

"That should make it easier, right?"

The woman shook her head sadly. "Your fat is under a layer of muscle. We can't access it."

I felt a little thrill at the suggestion I possessed stomach muscles. Maybe there was a six-pack inside the insulated cooler. "You can't slip in between them?"

"No, but thanks for stopping by."

And that was the extent of my consultation. Why that questionnaire couldn't be done online, I didn't know. Why the consult couldn't be done via Zoom was a mystery as well. What *wasn't* a mystery? The fact that under "Occupation" I'd written "Cashier."

I suspected that was my real diagnosis. Or maybe it was my answer to a different question: "What is your main goal for losing weight?"

I'd written, "I want to see my penis more easily." Bill Maher might be jerk, and shaming wasn't helpful, but I did want a better view.

Accurate fat analysis or not, it was now clear I wasn't going to be getting any surgical assistance. I'd have to try pedaling a little more. Perhaps finally add one day of intermittent fasting per week to my schedule, reduce my insulin on those days and do a couple of extra finger pricks to make sure my glucose wasn't dropping too low. I was still rationing the two-week sensors. The last one had stopped working only five days in.

Maybe if I started quilting again, I could keep my meter beside the sewing machine, and whenever I accidentally stuck myself with a pin, I'd have the meter ready to go.

But it wasn't much fun quilting only for myself.

Perhaps I could donate a few finished quilts to a Latinx immigration organization.

I walked back past Prada and Gucci and Chanel and Neiman Marcus and waited for the 560 back to Renton. I'd just missed the last bus by two minutes, and this bus ran only every half hour.

A route for store employees, not shoppers.

I stood with my fingers in my ears to combat the deafening construction work across the street. A new high-rise condo was going up. It felt odd to remember not everyone was financially challenged.

When the bus arrived twenty-eight clang-filled minutes later, I sat in the same seat as before. For the return trip, it was in the shade.

I'd lost a total of five and a half pounds in the last several weeks, all on my own. At this rate…I'd never live long enough to drop from obese even down to fat. When I stepped off the bus in the Renton Transit Center to wait for the 106, I grabbed a lemon-flavored protein bar. These were the good ones because they tasted like lemon-flavored cardboard. Just one and I lost my appetite every time.

Ten minutes later, I boarded the bus. The Native American driver who hated me coughed into his mask as I tapped my card, glaring at me as if I'd somehow been responsible. After another twenty minutes, I pulled the cord for my stop in Rainier Beach.

Even the sidewalk here felt like home.

***

I wore my bright red compression sleeves today. I'd pedaled on my bike this morning while watching the Weather Channel. Wildfires were approaching Lake Tahoe.

I remembered the days when meteorologists talked about rain and snow. Or beach weather. Reminded us to wear sunblock. Or to make sure our water pipes were winterized.

The last time it had snowed in Seattle, I wondered if that was the last time I would see snow.

Work had gone OK today. Gail was out sick. And now I was heading home, where I hoped to pedal some more while watching another episode of *Crime Scene Cleaner*.

A German comedy about a guy who cleans up the mess left by dead bodies.

I'd had to run to catch the 11, missed it, then walked up to where I could catch the 8 heading to Capitol Hill, missed that as well, and crossed the street to catch the 8 heading to Mount Baker instead. I was less attentive on the bus than usual, or trying to be, except that a black man probably in his early forties kept flirting with a black teenager maybe fifteen.

"Wanna have my baby?"

"Wanna go for a drink?"

"Wanna come to my place?"

Clever banter which the young woman completely ignored.

I frowned when the man followed her off, watching as the driver called the girl back. When she reboarded the bus, the man climbed back on, too. Then the driver told the girl, "Go straight home."

When the girl stepped off the bus again, the driver closed the doors and took off before the man could follow.

I jotted a quick note to commend the driver to Metro when I got home.

There was a reason Hitchcock didn't direct a film called *Strangers on a Bus*. But I did worry about casually meeting someone who turned out to be dangerous. And who would now know my route to work or what neighborhood I lived in.

That still didn't justify what I'd said to Tommy this morning.

"One day, you like me," Tommy had said as we waited for the bus, "and the next, you act like I have cooties."

"You're right," I said. "I'm nervous."

"Why?"

"Because I find you attractive but I'm not sure what to make of you."

"You think I'm crazy?"

"Tommy, I can tell you're neurodivergent." Was that even the right term? Maybe it was neuroatypical or something else. "I'm just not sure what kind of neurodivergent you are."

He put his hands on his hips. "Do I seem violent?"

I shook my head.

"Then why do you care 'what kind of neurodivergent' I am?"

He was no dummy.

"Because I was beaten up by a charming stalker once," I told him. A guy I'd met on the 49 ages ago, back when the University district still had half a dozen Used Book stores. He'd seen me board with my bag of previously read novels and offered to let me choose something from his home library. "I've even got coffee and scones," he added, "if it takes you a while to look through everything." His eyes had twinkled with such charm.

Richard had not been pleased when I finally left him three years and four STDs later.

At least three of the infections had been curable. And the bruises from our last encounter eventually healed.

Tommy stared at me for a long moment before responding. "You think I'm charming?" he asked, reaching over to pinch my nipple. "That's the nicest thing anyone's ever said to me."

"Uh…"

"I'm going to suck you off right here." He dropped to his knees and reached for my zipper.

"The bus is coming, Tommy. Let's do this another time."

Like never.

***

An elderly white man in clean blue jeans, a flannel shirt, and a fleece vest walked barefoot through the oil and broken glass of the transit center carrying a tiny yellow guitar.

For some reason, it made me want to sing, "Tip Toe Through the Tulips."

***

I'd just run across MLK from the light rail station to try to catch the 106, but it pulled off when I was still two yards from the bus shelter.

"Cazzo!"

At least I hadn't pulled anything. I walked the rest of the way to the pole where the schedules were posted, keeping enough distance so that others could check the timetables but close enough to be able to board quickly when the next bus arrived.

An elderly black man on the other side of Henderson started crossing the street. Not using a crosswalk, of course. And stepping off the curb into the turning lane so that he had four lanes of traffic to battle.

At half a mile an hour.

A young Latina teenager coming out of the Mexican grocery on the corner set her bag down and ran out into the street. She took the man by the arm and guided him the rest of the way across, shielding him when a car approached. Cars began backing up in both directions, but the young woman walked slowly and steadily alongside the old man until he safely reached the sidewalk.

Then she picked up her bag and continued on her way.

I'd just stood at the bus stop and watched, while this young woman went out in the street and did.

Last night, I'd made phone calls for SURJ—Showing Up for Racial Justice—but fundraising wasn't one of my strong points. It was pretty much the same thing as marketing. The difference between selling a product and making it.

I needed to stop being a passenger on my journey through life and get behind the wheel.

When another 106 pulled up a few minutes later, I climbed aboard and found a seat near the rear exit. A middle-aged Asian woman across from me spoke loudly on the phone with her mask down around her chin.

I didn't know what to do.

***

I'd spent the day quilting. More or less.

Maybe once a year, I tried to make the long trip up to Marysville to talk about quilting with a guy I'd met on Capitol Hill two decades earlier. Michael and his husband had moved to Marysville almost eight years ago now. Even when Brigham had been willing to drive me, that was a trip we couldn't make often.

And now…

There was the 106 to light rail, light rail downtown, the 512 to Everett, the 212 to Marysville, and then a ten-minute walk through 1970s suburbia. Three and a half hours one way. About thirty-five miles.

Almost faster to fly to Chicago.

Today, I watched Michael work on a new quilt for his church fundraiser and listened to him repeat stories of how he'd met Dean in the bushes of Volunteer Park. Time spent casually socializing around beautiful fabrics seemed the stuff of gods. When the two men hugged me goodbye and planted thoroughly platonic kisses on my cheek, I felt a satisfying rush of energy as if I'd eaten a cold, crisp piece of key lime pie.

On the 512 heading south to Seattle, I sat in the upper level of the double-decker bus. Fewer passengers up here—none at the moment—and a front row seat with an expansive view ahead.

Even the vacation Brigham and I had taken to Neah Bay hadn't been as restorative.

The double decker stopped at a freeway station between the northbound and southbound lanes, and I heard someone clomping up the steps to the second level. A heavyset black man swung into the seat across from me, gave me a quick once-over, and pulled down his mask.

"Want a hand job?" he asked. "Before anyone boards at the next stop?" He positioned the mask back over his nose.

I stood and crossed the aisle to sit next to him.

A couple of hours later, I was home. Looking at the picture the man had let me take of him with my phone, I grabbed a sheet of graph paper and started designing a quilt depicting what we'd done despite the security camera watching our every move.

Chapter Twelve: Are We There Yet?

My shift at the supermarket had been interrupted by a customer with a can punch, using the pointy end to poke holes in almost three dozen cans before anyone noticed.

"If you want to steal, then steal!" I'd shouted at him. "But don't ruin things for everyone else!"

The offending customer, a thin white man in his fifties, lunged at me with the can opener, and I jumped to the side. I was more worried about tetanus than the stab wound itself, though I was up to date with all my vaccinations.

My grandma's older sister had died of "lockjaw," a condition so horrifying that anyone who'd witnessed it would run any risk to avoid it. It began like a charley horse. But instead of your calf or your foot muscles contracting and causing intense pain for fifty or sixty seconds, the charley horse could start in your jaw or your neck…and never ended.

More and more muscles would join in, contracting so painfully that any single one of the contractions could make the infected person scream in pain.

But the contractions still wouldn't stop. More and more muscles kept joining in over the course of several hours, the agony unending.

Until finally, the heart muscle contracted, too, or the muscles controlling the person's breathing, and that was the end of that.

The customer lunged again and snagged my shirt. Odd that he seemed less threatening because he was wearing a mask. But that metal had come close.

I used the one martial arts move I'd learned in the Young Men's program at church and forced the guy's hand into a shelving unit. He shouted and dropped his weapon. He lunged at me again, and I repeated the self-defense maneuver with a bit more conviction.

This time, it looked like the guy broke a finger.

After I filled out the incident report and gave my statement to the police, Gail sent me home an hour early. I missed my first bus by fifteen seconds and then my transfer, but I didn't care.

More annoying was the heat, sweltering even at this time of day. The Earth had just recorded its hottest July on record.

Violent crime grew worse when it was hot.

I was glad I wouldn't be around in twenty years.

But I was here now. I tried to clear my mind of the incident at the store and ignore the Latino day laborer coughing four rows up. I'd be home soon. I'd take a chewable zinc tablet, and I'd watch an episode of *Murder In.* The one up next was set in Lorraine.

I caught a whiff of urine and saw a trickle of water passing under my seat. I lifted my legs and waited for the stream to finish.

When I'd transferred from Napoli to Rome late in my mission, I could only afford the cheapest train ticket. I'd had to sit on the floor in front of the bathroom the entire trip.

That was the day I learned the word "potabile" in Italian.

If I was being honest, that was the day I learned the word "potable" in English, too.

Today, I'd learned the word "apriscatole," looking it up while waiting for the police.

Brigham would never learn it.

***

I didn't believe in vampires, but something supernatural seemed to occur late in the day. Passengers could be crazy virtually any time, but they seemed to get just a bit crazier as evening approached. By 7:00, an hour most car owners still considered early, bus riders could encounter pretty much anything.

As the 7 headed south along Rainier, I watched a tall, heavyset black man one row up trying to fasten a watch around his wrist. When he decided he wasn't going to succeed, he tried selling the watch first to me and then to an Indian man, offering a produce bag filled with individually packaged condoms as an additional temptation. A white woman, around forty, with short shorts, bleached blond hair, and bloodshot eyes, boarded a stop or two later. She chewed something noisily with her mouth open, her face unmasked. And spit something she didn't like against the window.

A black woman in her thirties boarded with at least six bags, so many that she had to get off and climb on again with the last of them. She looked weary and unhappy, no surprise there, but when she got off the bus several stops later, she beat the side of the bus three times in frustration as the vehicle pulled off.

A black teenage girl sat across from me and kept pulling boogers out of her nose and wiping them on the seat next to her as she played on her cell phone. A white man in dress slacks, a white shirt, with a T-shirt underneath—was he Mormon?—sat up front in the disability section. He put his backpack and zippered lunch bag on the seats next to him, taking up the entire bench, and wouldn't move any of it when an elderly Latina boarded and had nowhere else to sit.

An Asian man in his fifties, drunk, sang The Partridge Family's "I Think I Love You."

I was impressed he knew the words.

Thank God it stayed light late during the summer. The bus was even crazier than this once the sun went down.

***

"What were you here for?" the woman asked. Totally inappropriate and invasive, of course, but friendly.

The woman was white, around forty, no more than a few pounds overweight. Her hair might have originally been brown but was now three different shades of blue. Other than that, she looked dressed for the office. I could tell the clothes were expensive because her blouse carried twice the usual number of buttons.

"A1C," I said. "You?"

"Ah, my husband's diabetic," she said, reaching out to touch my elbow but stopping herself. "I was here today for my knee." She lifted her skirt and shook her foot like Claudette Colbert in *It Happened One Night.*

"What's wrong with your knee?"

"I've had a ganglion cyst for three years."

"Ugh," I said. "I got one squeezing too hard on the clippers trimming vegetation back from the sidewalk." I wiggled my right thumb.

"Turned out this was actually cancer."

"Oh."

She shrugged. "Still seems to be localized, but they'll do more tests to verify."

I held up two crossed fingers. What could I say that wouldn't sound trite? "If your husband's been putting off cleaning the gutters or taking a few vacation days so you can do something fun together, now's the time to call it in."

She nodded, and that seemed to be the end of the conversation. I looked down the street, but no bus was in sight. "And what *is* your A1C?" the woman asked.

Nice.

I wondered if it would be inappropriate to ask her and her husband to dinner somewhere that offered outdoor seating. "I've been keeping it around 6.5, but I can't seem to get it much lower." Of course, friendly chatter to pass the time waiting for a bus didn't mean someone wanted to be your BFF.

"6.5 isn't bad."

"I don't keep track as well as I should." I shrugged. "Can't stand pricking my fingers twice a day." As if other folks loved such things.

The woman nodded. "Andy's the same way. I have to give him an incentive."

I frowned, though she couldn't see it underneath my mask.

"Why do you think I accepted that this was just a ganglion cyst for so long?" She pointed.

I laughed. "You did not just say that."

"You have a friend who can perhaps…distract you twice a day?" I could hear the smile in her voice though I couldn't see her lips, either. "You can count down together. One…two…three…jab! And both poke at the same time."

She bucked her hips the way Tommy sometimes did. I wasn't sure what to think. "Now that's an idea I could get behind," I managed.

"Or in front of, as the case may be."

I couldn't help but laugh, but when the bus arrived a moment later, we sat in different sections of the bus.

***

Non sapevo chi era quest'uomo, ma stavamo camminando insieme per un bel po'.

"Attento!" lui ha detto improvvisamente. "Api!"

Something woke me up then, and I returned to reality instantly. The bus was passing the home improvement store, where a dozen Latinos chatted with one another on the sidewalk while waiting for someone to offer them a job for the day.

"Cazzo!"

I'd missed my stop. I leaped from my seat and hurried out the exit before the bus moved on and I would have an even longer walk back to my transfer point.

***

Earbud day.

I kept my eyes closed, peeking for a couple of seconds during each song, both to make sure I stayed awake and to keep track of where I was along the route.

But it was hard to pay attention to anything else when Christian sang, "Un'altra vita, un altro amore."

Just as difficult, but for completely different reasons, when Tuto Cotugno sang, "L'italiano."

Bobby Solo's "Tu stai" was beautiful in yet another way.

As was Giuseppe Cionfoli's "Solo Grazie."

Rino Martinez, though, singing, "Biancaneve," was fun and ridiculous and mesmerizing and beautiful all at the same time. I kept remembering where I was in Rome the night he performed in the San Remo music festival, dressed in what amounted to a cerulean superhero outfit.

I'd wanted to marry him on the spot, though I could hardly express such sentiments to my missionary companion or the devout Catholic family sharing their television with us that evening.

On our fifth anniversary, Brigham had come out of the bedroom wearing a similar outfit, though the white boots weren't quite a perfect match. But he'd been watching the YouTube video and working with a friend to recreate the costume.

I was legally married to Brigham but his gift to me that night was an evening of wild sex with "Rino."

For years afterward, Brigham would periodically show up for Date Night in his Biancaneve outfit. Underneath, he wore his one-piece Mormon underwear.

We might have been thoroughly fucked up, but we had a good time at it.

The bus pulled into the Mount Baker Transit Center. Only three passengers were left on board by this point, one a thin, black woman who'd been sitting on the back row. When she followed me off the bus and coughed, I turned around to see that she wore nothing other than a shirt that didn't quite cover her private parts.

Chapter Thirteen: All Roads Lead to Rome

I jogged down the first two flights of steps, but then I heard the train pulling up, so I slammed my Orca card against the reader, waited impatiently for the beep, and ran down the last flight of steps, rushing through the doors just in time…

To hear the conductor announce, "All passengers please deboard the train."

It was then I noticed the cute Latino. He either understood enough English to follow the muffled announcement or could see enough movement to realize others were getting off the train. A huge crowd stood on the platform, close to a hundred people from the four cars. It was going to be a challenge piling into the next train that would already hold just as many passengers before it even arrived.

"So much for social distancing," I said to the Latino. Brilliant. Hysterical.

A black woman nearby with a chador wore a T-shirt that read, "Team Human." An unmasked white couple with two suitcases on wheels moaned about missing their flight.

It was a legitimate worry. Odd that their failure to wear masks extinguished whatever sympathy I might otherwise have felt for them.

Which didn't say much for my character. Their plight was still real.

"I just want to go home," the Latino said. I thought of the Beach Boys song I used to sing to myself during my first days in Italy.

Another muffled announcement came over the loudspeaker. There'd been an "incident," and the southbound platforms from Capitol Hill to SODO would be out of use "temporarily." We were to climb up the stairs, cross over the mezzanine, and go down the steps to the other side of the building. Trains on the northbound platform would alternate between north and south.

"Did you get all that?" I asked.

"We need to cross to the other side."

And now I was thinking about *Man's Search for Happiness*. And *Poltergeist*.

Throngs of riders headed for the stairs, a few running to the elevator and pressing the button for the mezzanine so quickly that no one else had a chance of entering with them.

"Do you want to take my elbow?" I asked. "It might be faster."

The Latino's eyes seemed to meet mine, and I again wondered what level of vision he had. He nodded.

"Would you rather the elevator or the stairs?"

"The elevator."

Made sense, just to avoid the mass of people bumping into one another. The unmasked couple with the suitcases was waiting by the doors, along with several other folks. I was tempted to kiss the Latino in hopes of making the tourists uncomfortable enough to move away but didn't.

We weren't able to get on the next elevator but did board the one after that. Inside the car, the Latino maneuvered to a position behind me against the back wall, and I had to be careful not to let the others cramming in after us smash me against him. I felt the man's hand move from my elbow to my waist as he pulled me back, and I let my ass press against his crotch.

I felt a little twitch from his pants.

"Sorry," he whispered into my ear.

"I'm not," I whispered back.

The doors opened and we made our way across the mezzanine, dodging the last of the others coming over from the stairs. "My name's Todd," I said.

"Rocio."

"Pleasure to feel you," I said. "I mean, meet you."

"You're bad."

"You should see what I'm like in private."

"I have sensitive fingertips," Rocio said. He had a definite accent, but he spoke crisply, without struggling.

"Any other sensitive areas?"

"Two or three."

No one seemed to need the elevator going down. Most folks had already reached the northbound platform by this point, and the others seemed OK with walking down stairs they hadn't been willing to climb. So it was just the two of us in the elevator.

"I almost want to kiss you in here," Rocio said.

"I almost want to…" I stopped myself from saying anything too inappropriate.

The northbound platform had already been crowded with folks heading north, and with all of us mixing in, I was grateful most of them were wearing masks. I had flashbacks of a rally at Westlake the previous year and another in Rainier Beach.

The first train to arrive headed north. I debated boarding and heading to the University of Washington, one stop past the closed Capitol Hill platform, and then coming back on the southbound train, but such a trip would easily add another twenty minutes to my commute, and it seemed too hard to navigate with a blind man. I certainly wasn't going to leave him this soon.

"You just getting off?" I asked.

He smirked. "I work in a dental office around the corner."

I hated to admit I wondered what a blind employee could do there. I really needed to educate myself. Since I didn't want to show my ignorance, I remained ignorant and asked another question. "What do you do for fun?"

"You get right to the point, don't you?"

"I meant..." But I didn't really know what I'd meant. I reached into my wallet and pulled out the slip of paper with my name and phone number. "Let me give you this before I forget."

Rocio took the paper, held it an inch from his face, and put it in his own wallet. He didn't give me his number in return.

Ten minutes later, another northbound train pulled into the station. By this point, Rocio and I had discussed movies and music. He liked Almodóvar, Selena, and Laura Pausini.

"I like Pausini, too," I said. "I listen to her Italian songs."

Just as I began to worry we'd run out of things to talk about and be left standing awkwardly next to each other, a southbound train arrived. Over on the southbound tracks.

The crowd of those waiting to head south had grown to a hundred and fifty by this point, and dozens of people rushed for the stairs to the mezzanine while others made a dash for the elevators, as if acting out the "Flight 209 now arriving at Gate 8" scene from *Airplane!* Rocio took my elbow again and we headed for the elevator as well, finally managing to squeeze inside three trips later.

He maneuvered himself against the back wall and pulled me into his crotch again. "Lo siento," he said. I remembered the phrase from one of the Spanish shows I'd watched on MHz.

"No soy." With my accent, it sounded like I was ordering coffee.

***

Anti-maskers had threatened health officials at a school board meeting in Tennessee and a dozen other states. Nurses were being provided panic buttons because of the rising number of assaults. Doctors were receiving death threats.

Protesters—I couldn't even keep track of where—had hung a banner demanding the White House "Free the J6 Political Prisoners!"

Investigators had found the remains of hundreds of Native children on boarding school grounds in Canada from the days of forced deculturization.

It had been a relief when a screw fell out of my eyeglass frames yesterday morning, a lens followed suit, and I'd gone an entire day without being able to read the news. But I did want to see clearly, so today I was heading to Capitol Hill to fix my frames.

The black man in the seat in front of me took up the usual two seats but also took up the two seats across the aisle from him with a second bag. When three new riders boarded, another black man somewhere behind me called out.

"Hey," he said. "Be cool. Move your bag off those seats so other people can sit down."

The man in the row ahead of me clearly understood the comment was directed at him. He turned to look behind me with an expressionless face and then turned up his music. Hip hop lyrics so loud they could be heard throughout the bus blasted from his earphones. The bus driver looked in her rearview mirror.

Better to be irritated by this passenger, I reminded myself, than to be him. It was a mantra I repeated as often as necessary, two or three times a day.

Or four or five or…

We passed an ice cream shop. In the front window was a hand-painted sign. "Look out for each other."

***

Would this summer never end? The closest shade was too far from the bus stop to risk using. It was still early morning, and already my armpits were damp. My crotch, too. I'd managed to prevent any jock itch this year, but it was a constant battle. The new underwear I'd bought a few weeks back helped, with cloth barriers to better help separate my dick and balls from the rest of my skin.

The boxer briefs were bright blue and bright red and bright green, just in case I ever had the chance to let anyone see them.

For a year and a half now, I'd been carrying a tiny bottle of hand sanitizer with me, but last week, I'd started carrying single pack wipes designed for "sensitive skin."

You know, like dicks and assholes.

Even if I never used them for that purpose, knowing I *could* accept any invitation felt liberating.

***

A black man in his fifties, with henna red hair and wearing a caftan, boarded the bus. I wondered if he colored his pubic hair.

Did faiths other than Mormonism have religious underwear?

We passed a law office specializing in car accidents and workplace injuries. Then senior living apartments, a pho restaurant, and several homeless tents near the tennis center.

A police car drove past.

Newscasts were reporting that many officers across the country were resigning rather than be vaccinated. An obnoxious right-wing pundit claimed that "the mandate" was created specifically to identify sincere Christians, free thinkers, and men with high testosterone so they could be kicked out of the military.

The actual mandate allowed people to opt out of vaccination if they agreed to weekly testing.

I was fine with military and police officers self-selecting to leave, given the high correlation between anti-vaxxers and other problematic attitudes. I'd known several Democrats over the years who'd been anti-vaxxers, too, but it had been hit or miss before. Now hating vaccines had become right-wing religious dogma.

A thin black woman in her fifties scrambled aboard the bus at the next stop with a broken umbrella. There wasn't a cloud in the sky. She brandished it like a sword as she approached.

"Stop looking at me!" she yelled.

I complied, though I tried to guard myself from sudden attack using my peripheral vision.

"We are all enlisted now until the conflict is o'er." The lyrics from the old church hymn bounced around in my head.

Brigham's favorite dessert was coffee cake with coffee, to prove he was no longer trapped.

A person transitioned from old to senile, I remembered reading somewhere, when they spent more time reminiscing than living.

Chapter Fourteen: Waiting by the Side of the Road

I thought for a moment. I did need social interaction, was obviously desperate for it, and I could use ASL in practically any job. Hell, as difficult as it was to hear through masks, it would be helpful even for folks with full hearing ability to know some sign language.

Elders Johanson and Fielding looked at me expectantly. Stopping by the Mount Baker Transit Center to spread the gospel.

I remembered how boring and stressful missionary work could be. It was difficult to be in sales when you knew almost no one was interested in your product.

But American Sign Language? Now *that* was a product worth promoting. I'd learned the alphabet after reading *The Happy Hollisters and the Haunted House Mystery* when I was nine. Learned a few phrases and the words to "I am a Child of God" in the Single Adults group when an elderly deaf widow was baptized.

"You OK with sitting in the back yard?" I asked. "I only have two chairs on my front porch, but I can set out three in back when you come over."

"Hmm," Elder Johanson murmured. "We'll want to start with a prayer, so..."

"No need for that. Language instruction is plenty." And they didn't need to know I was ex-Mormon.

The two young men glanced at each other. They were the only two ASL missionaries in the area, they'd told me, covering three distinct missions. Back in the day, I'd never been allowed outside my zone, much less my mission. I even had to get special permission to go sight-seeing in Rome if the Coliseum or Vatican wasn't in my assigned area. Down in Napoli, no missionary was allowed permission to visit Pompeii.

You couldn't convert dead people, after all. Baptize them, perhaps, but only if you knew their names, and that was taken care of by genealogists.

"We can wear masks indoors," Elder Fielding assured me.

To be fair, that wasn't nothing. I'd seen a news video of a Utahn aboard a flight from Los Angeles to Salt Lake ranting and growling like a dog, shoving his mask in his mouth, and demanding his right to...God only knew what was going through a mind like that. So these ASL teachers were perhaps salvageable as temporary friends.

"Which vaccine did you get?" I asked. "You both get the same kind?"

Elder Johanson shook his head. "We have a religious exemption," he explained. "Besides, we're young and healthy."

I stuck out my index finger and thumb at right angles while curling my other fingers against my palm.

"I see you know some sign language already."

I then spelled "I," followed by "A" and then "R."

Both missionaries frowned.

"President Nelson has come out publicly, at least twice, in support of vaccinations," I said.

"You know who President Nelson is?"

"If you want to say you're avoiding the vaccine for personal reasons, then say it. But don't use religion as a cover for your behavior."

"Our religion gives us freedom of choice."

"Then it's still *your* decision, isn't it, not God's."

"Well…"

"I think I'll just watch some ASL videos on YouTube."

"It's not the same."

Elder Johanson was right about that.

I wanted to tell them they were being assholes, call them apostates for following the Republican religion more than their own. And then compliment them on their ties, praise their haircuts, tell them I was practicing net zero cursing.

I wondered if they even knew who Greta Thunberg was.

When the 8 pulled up a moment later, I turned around on the bottom step and used one of the few phrases I remembered how to sign. "Thank you."

I wasn't even sure why I said it.

***

Rocio's belt buckle was embossed with the letters "VL." Whatever they might have stood for, it wasn't "Very Large." Still, he'd been quite enthusiastic while using several different body parts for various activities, and we'd had a good time.

Rather, *I'd* had a good time.

I could see the light rail pulling away now from Seatac Airport. It would reach the Tukwila station within a minute. We were elevated here as well, and the two stops were probably only a quarter mile apart.

When the doors opened, I stepped in and searched for a seat. Even this late in the evening, the car was half full, mostly with tourists and their baggage. I was relieved to see that many of the visitors wore face masks. I found a seat near the rear of the car and stared out the window.

"Would you like to do this again?" I'd asked Rocio while we dressed afterward.

"Well…" he said, and that was all the answer I needed. "I'm moving in with my boyfriend next week. He wouldn't like knowing you'd been here tonight, but I wanted to play one more time."

It didn't even matter if it was true. Either way, I wished I'd been a better toy for him tonight. I'd lost almost seven pounds now, but that was like scooping a bucket of sand off the beach and expecting someone to notice.

The light rail sped along the elevated track, rocking back and forth so violently I feared it would derail. The runaway subway in *The Taking of Pelham One Two Three*. No one else seemed bothered. The gap between Tukwila and Rainier Beach was the longest so far between any stops and could take almost ten minutes. I watched cars speeding by in both directions on the freeway below, looked at the lights from Southcenter Mall, spotted a wooden dock along the Duwamish.

A single tourist, male, dragging a small suitcase, walked into the car through the narrow passage connecting it to the other half. He had indeterminate features, perhaps Persian, maybe Indian, possibly Latino, made harder to discern because of his mask. I supposed it was colorist of me, but I loved his medium light brown skin.

The guy was almost certainly gay, with his jeans tailored to show every vein in his dick. He'd need a belt buckle that said "XL" at the very least.

The man caught my eye briefly, but since I was usually invisible to men with bodies like that, the split second was plenty. He stood leaning against the wall near the doors, positioned to give me a direct line of sight. He didn't look at me again, but he shifted every twenty or thirty seconds as if modeling a new Fall collection.

Perhaps an "XXL" belt buckle.

I wondered if any enterprising designers had come up with a gay line. Maybe "M/M" or "8" or even the blatant "Top."

The man shifted again.

Cazzo!

Literally.

I wondered if it would be OK to continue fantasizing about Rocio even if I knew he wasn't fantasizing about me in return, or if that would be too pathetic.

The light rail rounded the last curve coming into Rainier Beach and slowly descended to ground level, passing a construction yard, a storage facility, and a church. I waited until the train stopped before I stood and made my way to the door.

"Thanks, buddy," I said to the generous tourist as I passed him on my way out.

Chapter Fifteen: Il Capolinea del Cuore

Years ago, I'd signed up with Jewish Family Services to volunteer with the elderly. I was still in my forties then and "elderly" was such a distant concept as to seem alien. I'd been given a peach assignment, to play pool with a ninety-five-year-old man twice a month.

The guy lived with his grandson in Queen Anne, and everyone he knew had grown tired of playing with him. But I loved the game, had even been part of the High Heel league at one point, though I'd never been particularly skilled. The assignment sure beat grocery shopping for a crotchety senior or accompanying someone to medical appointments.

The problem had been the commute, only an hour by bus but, because the family lived in an exclusive neighborhood, their home lay an additional fifteen-minute walk from the nearest stop. The stroll was lovely—beautiful Tudors, exquisitely landscaped yards, and spectacular views of the city—unless it was raining or thirty-five degrees and windy.

Charles liked to play for at least two hours, so by the time a three-hour commute was added in, the visit, while thoroughly enjoyable, consumed five hours of my day off.

I'd eventually dropped my visits to once a month. Charles began missing shots on purpose to extend each game, afraid I was avoiding him because I lost every time. I felt like a putz when I told him I couldn't come back and play with him anymore.

***

An elderly Asian woman wearing a conical bamboo hat boarded at MLK and Othello. If there was ever a time to culturally appropriate fashion, it was during this unending heat wave.

All I could do for now was hold up the book I was reading as a shield against the uncomfortable rays beaming through the window. *Caste*. A customer at work had suggested it while I scanned her coupons.

I almost asked her to watch a new Sara Martins show with me.

***

OK. I was doing this. I locked my front door and headed to the bus stop. It was my day off, and I was voluntarily choosing to ride as many buses as I could stomach.

Wearing a T-shirt that said "Consenting Adult" on the front and "Just Say Yes" on the back.

The muscular Asian driving the 106 did a double take as I boarded but didn't shout Hallelujah and immediately hand over his phone number. I realized if I sat down, no one else might even be able to read the shirt, so I stood near the rear exit.

I was wide as a billboard.

I rode the 48 next. Then the 49, the 43, the 10, and the 8.

My feet were killing me.

Oh, well, I thought as we pulled into the Mount Baker Transit Center, it had been worth a shot. I could always cut up the shirt and make panels for a T-shirt quilt.

I stepped off the bus with the last of the passengers and started heading toward Rainier. As I passed the front door, the driver called out. "Hey! Hey, you!"

I turned to look. The guy, with skin slightly darker than mine, was unimpressive at first glance, short, pudgy, bald, even the visible portion of his face suggesting unattractive features. He didn't give off a single gay vibe, though it was possible I'd just refused to consider them.

"Yes?" Maybe he was going to lecture me.

"Where I get a shirt like that?" The man had a thick Asian accent, though I couldn't narrow it down any more specifically than that.

"It's one of a kind," I said. "I had it made special."

"I want give one to my girlfriend."

Oh.

"I let you suck me, you give me that shirt?"

So magnanimous. But that honestly *did* sound like a good deal. I headed toward the comfort station to meet him when he deboarded.

A few minutes later, I walked across Rainier shirtless, advertising my obesity with every jiggling step, and waited for the 106 back home.

An elderly homeless man, white and unmasked, pushing a grocery cart of belongings, stopped on his way down the sidewalk. After rummaging through a torn garbage bag for a moment, he handed me a dirty Seahawks shirt. Scabies and lice and other cooties crawling through my mind, I accepted the shirt and pulled it on.

The widower's mite.

***

A white woman in her forties boarded the bus. Very, very slowly, waddling along a few inches at a time.

Shuffling. Shuffling was a nicer word. The woman must have weighed close to 350 pounds. She wasn't using a walker but held onto every possible surface within reach until she plopped down on the bench in the disability section so heavily I worried it might collapse, like a scene out of *Shallow Hal*.

I found myself absentmindedly rubbing my stomach, stopping when I felt a lump.

Even if a guy wasn't put off by my weight, he almost certainly would find my lumpiness objectionable. Both thighs and my stomach were covered with lumps. Some were temporary—bruises—but others were pretty much permanent, lipohypertrophy or even scar tissue from injecting in the same areas too often.

I kept a map and rotated, but after so many thousands of injections, the lumps were almost impossible to avoid.

And who'd be interested in a warthog?

I looked out the window and sighed. We passed a pawn shop and a billiard hall and a long stretch of campers and RVs where unhoused folks still tried to survive.

A newlywed lesbian couple camping near Moab had been murdered the other day.

I fingered another lump, this one on my thigh.

Brigham had been interested. At least some of the time. He'd taken to wearing a sleep mask the last couple of years when we had sex so he could concentrate on the body of the man in his fantasies rather than mine, but I understood he couldn't help being influenced by media messaging any more than I could.

Just like black people could buy into concepts of inferiority, fat people couldn't help hearing hundreds of social messages a day telling us we were lazy and weak and stupid. If I was *really* a strong, competent person, I'd find *some* way to lose this weight.

Internalized fat shaming. Or a form of cultural appropriation. I had appropriated a moral code from the dominant culture that oppressed overweight folks.

Too bad intellectualizing a problem didn't solve it.

Even as a staunch Mormon, I'd never thought poorly of openly gay men. If anything, I was jealous. I thought *I* was bad for not being able to "overcome" my orientation, but I didn't think other people were failures.

Of course, that just amounted to arrogance. Somehow, despite my self-loathing and self-doubt, I still thought of myself as better than most gays and therefore expected *I* could achieve something others couldn't.

As a white person I tried to confront my racial biases but still inadvertently perpetuated racism. As a fat person, I continually perpetuated fat shaming while not meaning to.

I was Emily Litella upset that folks were complaining about "violins on television."

A heavyset Polynesian man on the sidewalk glanced at the bus as we passed. I'd do *him*, I thought. Some heavy men were attractive and some weren't. And lots of thinner men certainly weren't.

Though that probably involved other unconscious biases.

Was asymmetrical bias a thing?

A black woman in a hijab, sporting bright yellow eyeglasses, exited a building with a Now Leasing sign in front. She walked past a retaining wall covered with thousands of bicycle reflectors.

We passed a 30-foot green shovel installed near the Columbia City station. I remembered dozens of elaborate murals along the tracks in SODO.

South Seattle was just full of culture.

I supposed my fat stomach was part of it. At least I was wearing a fun mask today—Mt. Rainier covered in snow, designed by a local Suquamish artist.

***

"I've been waiting for half an hour!" An elderly white woman smacked the plexiglass door protecting the driver as she boarded the bus. She was lying, of course. I'd gone out early this morning to make sure I caught the bus with Tommy, so I'd seen the previous bus go by before I boarded this one.

Still, I understood how she felt. Transit funding showed up on the ballot fairly often. One of the rare arguments I'd had with Brigham had been over one such property tax measure.

"It's a regressive tax," he'd said. "I can't support regressive taxes. They hurt the poorest people."

"Unless you can get a morally acceptable funding measure on the ballot in two days," I said, "this is what we have."

"When it doesn't pass, the mayor and city council will decide to find a better way to fund transit on the next ballot."

"And in the years before that happens, the 'poorest people' will have to deal with longer wait times between buses. Every day."

"Well—"

"I'm going to pay for this one way or the other," I said. "I'd just as soon get a better bus system when I pay."

"But it's a problem no matter how we pay for it," Brigham insisted. "If we make transit better, people with money end up moving into up-and-coming areas, so we really just contribute to gentrification. That pushes poor people farther from the things they need. It's better to leave the poor with bad transit."

I felt like an MRI machine, seeing into my partner's brain in a way I never had before. It wasn't that what he said wasn't true.

"So we're doing the poor a favor by keeping them miserable and oppressed?"

"Well…"

"Al povero mancano tante cose," I'd reminded him, "all'avaro tutte."

Brigham had still voted against the property tax increase. I'd voted for it. The measure had failed.

And the route I was taking at that time to commute to a job in White Center had added another fifteen minutes between buses. It took three buses to reach that job to begin with. The commute, already awful, became an absolute nightmare.

I'd bitched at my husband one last time when the election results were announced. "You have a lot of curiosity about a thousand different things," I'd said, "and that's truly impressive, but you're not the least bit interested in what life is like for those of us on public transit."

Brigham hadn't responded, but I could see his jaw tightening.

"When I get home from work," I continued to vent, "you ask about my day, and every day, part of what I talk about is the commute. So you *know* what it's like. It's just not important to you."

"That's not true."

"Well, it's important to me."

The bus pulled away from another stop after two passengers exited, but then a thirty-something black man banged on the window behind me so loudly I jumped. "Hey! I want out! Open the doors, motherfucker!"

The bus lurched to a stop again, the driver opened the rear exit, and the rider moved to leave. "Fuckin' racist!" he yelled, banging the doors on his way out.

The driver closed the doors and drove on.

Chapter Sixteen: The Road Less Traveled

I double-bagged the broken microwave and headed out the door. The nearest disposal location for electronics and kitchen appliances was in SODO. A long trip but mostly by light rail. I still had Brigham's old laptop to get rid of and a broken keyboard of my own.

And there was the half-empty can of polyurethane.

But that would require a separate trip to Haz Waste.

A well-dressed white woman boarded the bus on Rainier with her coffee and a doughnut. She wore a lovely Starry Night mask but pulled it down to take a bite of her doughnut, leaving it down below her chin as she chewed. Finally, she pulled her mask up again.

Until two seconds later when she pulled it down to take a sip of her coffee. But then, thank goodness, she pulled her mask back up again.

And then pulled it down to take another bite of her doughnut and chew.

Someone farted.

I got out on MLK and walked half a block back to Henderson. Once on the far side, I pushed another button to cross MLK.

When blind commuters heard the beeps and twitters, how did they know *which* direction was now safe?

A train pulled up while I was waiting for the Walk sign, which meant I had to stand for another entire light cycle. The train had long since headed north before I finally reached the platform.

A young white woman smoking weed fouled the air with dead skunk smell, so I moved down the platform until I reached the dinosaurs. A thirtyish Asian man joined me and began speaking loudly on his phone, unmasked, so I moved over to the Egyptian hieroglyphics.

This time of day, the train wasn't terribly crowded, and most folks wore masks, though an interracial couple in the seat across from me kept theirs below their nose.

"It's not a good luck charm," I said.

The man, white, flipped me off. The woman, Asian, pulled her mask below her lips as well, as if that were somehow more threatening. I kept looking at them calmly, not turning away, until they decided to move to another car.

Two Chinese tourists, both double-masked, were showing each other something on their phones. I remembered that just a few days earlier, there'd been horrific flooding in central China. Twelve people had drowned on a subway.

Of course, these tourists were probably from Cincinnati.

Coming around the corner into SODO, I scanned the homeless encampments, one on either side of the street, one right on top of apparently no longer used railroad tracks. A U.S. flag waved from the top of a tent.

Proudly? Ironically?

I wasn't sure it mattered.

I picked up my bags and exited at the next stop, crossing two bus lanes and heading on to a street lined with warehouses and other industrial buildings.

After dropping off my two items, I considered strolling through the neighborhood looking for some sweaty dick, but simply returning home with two empty bags was reward enough for the day.

***

"Thanks for the ride, Bruce."

"I couldn't let you miss the memorial, could I? Ramesh might come back as a murder hornet and get me."

That was the third Asian joke he'd made today. "What happens when you cross a dumb blonde with a Thai?" started the first and an allusion to Japanese internment camps was part of the next.

The Squad had decided to wait until the pandemic died down before gathering family and friends together, but it looked like it simply wasn't going to get better anytime soon, so we'd moved forward with the plans.

Bruce had been one of the last-minute members of the Squad, one of Ramesh's straight friends who barely knew Brigham. At least, I didn't remember Brigham ever mentioning him. I'd caught the bus to his place in Seward Park this morning, and now we'd boarded the ferry to Bainbridge Island. From there, we'd drive all the way to Chimacum for the service.

"Do you know why Chinese parents throw pots and pans in the air?" Bruce asked.

"I'd rather not hear the answer," I said. "I'm heading up to the deck." My departure was only a nominal success. Bruce followed me up the wet stairs. Dozens of people already sat at the tables chatting or reading.

An automated announcement reminded everyone that masks were mandatory.

I continued to the front, found an empty spot along the railing, and held on tight. Brigham and I used to lean against this railing and kiss every time we crossed.

"It's cold," Bruce noted.

"It's wonderful," I said. 90 degrees yesterday in Seattle and still chilly out on the water. Windy, too.

The Olympics towered in the distance, smaller than the Cascades on the Seattle side of the Sound but still impressive. Jellyfish floated just below the surface of the water. No orcas in sight, though a small pod had been spotted near the San Juans last week.

"I'm going back inside."

I didn't even turn to watch him leave. The cool, misty air and the jagged mountain range were too glorious.

Better than the image on the news of folks fleeing a Greek island, their ferry surrounded by flames.

A young Latino family lined against the railing for a photo.

Twenty minutes later, the Winslow waterfront grew clearer, and I headed back below deck. Several car alarms competed with one another for dominance. Bruce huddled in his car, shivering when I opened the door, and soon we followed the other cars on shore.

***

"Almost home," Bruce announced after we parked on a different ferry for the return to Seattle. The drive to Chimacum had seemed interminable, the memorial with its socializing before and catered meal after had consumed most of the day, and then there'd been the long, long drive back to Bainbridge in the growing haze of smoke. Though we'd eaten outdoors, with only three people to a table, and though I'd worn my mask the rest of the time, the afternoon had still been unnerving.

"I'm heading to the deck," I said.

"I'll wait here."

At this point, I really didn't even need Bruce. Once in Seattle, it would be only a short walk to light rail.

Bruce had lectured about *The Egg and I* as we drove through downtown Chimacum, i.e., a single intersection.

He spent half the day bragging about his successful import business, turning his back on the server who asked him a question about it, ignoring her when she repeated the question more loudly in case he simply hadn't heard.

The server was a friend of the host, who was another of Ramesh's friends, the original organizer of the Squad.

On the drive back to Winslow, Bruce had recounted every horror story he could remember about ferry disasters. One in Korea had killed three hundred. Another in Sweden had killed over eight hundred.

And one, he claimed, killed over four thousand in the Philippines.

Interesting that he'd chosen to remain below deck.

Preferable to my company, I supposed. Over the past year and a half, my diplomacy skills had dwindled like *The Incredible Shrinking Man*. I just didn't give a fuck what people thought anymore.

During the service, everyone had taken a turn sharing a memory of Ramesh before scooping some of his ashes into a wheelbarrow half-filled with compost and then mixing them in.

"One time when I went out with Ramesh and Brigham," I'd said, "the TV in the restaurant was too loud, so Ramesh pulled a universal remote out of his man-purse and clicked off the television."

Bruce's anecdote was about the time Ramesh had told him how impressed he was with Bruce's taste in clothing.

Ah, to be on the bus with Tommy again.

The Seattle waterfront was fast approaching, full of potential with the Viaduct demolished. I walked back below deck and joined Bruce.

“Thanks again for the ride.”

“Don’t get any ideas.”

After explaining he had an evening of work emails ahead of him, he dropped me off at the International District light rail station, and I tapped my card at the top of the stairs before heading to the platform.

Two white tourists, masked, waited just behind the yellow line with their suitcases, the woman wearing what looked like an expensive pashmina. Cerulean blue.

I missed Rino.

A white man, heavily tattooed and wearing a stained white T-shirt, stood ten feet away from them, singing, “I got murder on my mind,” over and over and over and over.

The woman’s husband leaned over the yellow line and peered down the tunnel, willing the train to arrive.

The house would be dark when I got home.

At least I had some homemade cookies to eat before bed, if I was willing to up my insulin. I’d spent some time with the server late in the afternoon to make up for Bruce’s diss. We’d talked about the plight of adjunct faculty and gig workers. Then she packed up some leftovers for me when it was time to leave.

Hosts often considered vegetarian options for guests but few seemed to remember carbs. Not their job, really, but disappointing regardless. Once, at my last workplace, we'd all had to attend a mandatory company dinner. The only safe item in the entire meal had been lettuce. So I'd pulled an emergency protein bar from my pocket.

"You'll never make it in this business," my supervisor had told me the following day. "You *embarrassed* me."

Had I been caught looking at someone's crotch?

"You *always* eat what you're served," he went on.

"I'm dia—"

"Winners don't ask for special accommodations. You make what you have work."

I was a reasonably intelligent man, but that didn't make me any more suited to life in a capitalist society than anyone else. That kind of success clearly required something I lacked. And didn't even understand.

It was like a deaf person wishing she could hear.

But if the only way to avoid succumbing to the siren call was not to hear it, I was OK with my disability.

Chapter Seventeen: Journey of a Thousand Bus Stops

Ida had grown from a Cat 3 to a Cat 4 in one hour, striking New Orleans on the 16th anniversary of Katrina. The music store where Louis Armstrong worked as a teen had collapsed. The Bed and Breakfast in the Marigny where Brigham and I stayed on our honeymoon had its roof ripped off.

Over fifty oil spills in the Gulf of Mexico. Reminding me of the revelation from the android in *Alien* that the crew had been expendable all along.

There was video from New York, where the remnants of Ida flooded the subways and streets, riders standing on bus seats, a geyser in a subway tunnel. A family of five drowned in their basement apartment in New Jersey.

Central Park had recorded an all-time record rainfall, over three inches in one hour, the week before Ida. This week, they beat that record.

Brigham and I had danced together at Bethesda Fountain.

Why hadn't I taken more pictures of Brigham on our rare vacations? Or working in our yard, or cooking dinner, or even taking a shower?

I was ready today, though. This time of morning, the driver with the shaved head and long white beard drove the 106. I'd snap a quick photo with my cell phone. It wouldn't be quite as presumptuous as asking him out but would let him know I was interested. If he didn't share the interest, I'd still have the photo for myself.

A smiling Latina opened the doors today. I nodded pleasantly, tapped my card, and headed for my seat.

***

"You gotta read it!" Tommy said, pressing the novel into my hands. *Smash and Grab* wasn't an appealing title, and the graffiti-style artwork reminded me too much of the parking lot at work.

"I'm a slow reader," I protested, hoping the threat of not getting his book back would make Tommy reconsider.

"It's about a fossil hunter who falls in love with a shapeshifter!"

"OK."

"The guy turns into a *dinosaur*!"

"It's a gay romance?" I asked, visions of the most bizarre bestiality possible flashing through my brain.

"You silly!" Tommy said, grabbing my crotch. "He's human when they fuck."

"Well…" I had to admit, the premise was intriguing.

"Why don't you ride the train with me to Tukwila and I'll read to you on the way? Then you can catch the train back and be a few minutes late for work."

Gail had already hinted yesterday she might be late this morning and had asked me to cover for her.

"We can even meet one bus earlier and do this again tomorrow."

Back during my Single Adult days at church, a proposal like this would have been considered a "service project." But now I felt like Bonnie Plunkett in *Mom* discovering that when you helped others you ended up helping yourself.

"Can you make good dinosaur noises?" I asked.

Tommy chirped like a bird and started pecking me on the neck. We boarded the 106 a few moments later, and he pecked and chirped all the way to the light rail station.

What was the point of being embarrassed anymore?

***

My phone pinged and I found a text from Makenna in Utah. "Salt Lake is drying up. It stinks."

I assumed she meant the lake rather than the city, though the options weren't mutually exclusive. "You good?" I texted back. "Everything fine here."

"Good if you like living in an asylum."

"LOL."

A white man in his late twenties boarded the bus, maskless, wearing a T-shirt that read, "Kiss me! I'm Italian!"

I motioned him over to my seat. He approached, his eyebrows furrowed. "I know you?" he asked. That five o'clock shadow was heart-stopping.

"Not yet," I told him. "I was just going to do what you asked." I pulled my mask down for two seconds and touched my lips. "Baciarti." I replaced my mask.

"Huh?"

I pointed to his shirt.

He looked down, realized what I was saying, and returned his gaze to me. "You got balls, dude."

I nodded. "Did you want to see?"

He frowned.

"Listen," I said, "you don't ruin my day with your unmasked kissable face, and I won't ruin yours with my gay lust. Deal?"

"Fucker."

"Are you propositioning me?"

The man glared, and I pointed up toward the front of the bus. "Masks are in the dispenser up there." When he still didn't move, I added, "Or did you want one of my used ones?" I started reaching into my back pocket.

He marched forward, grabbed a mask, and held it against his face as he passed by again. "Happy now?"

"I'm not asking you to donate a kidney," I said. "I'm just asking you to be a decent human being." But then, maybe that was an even harder request.

The man clomped his way to the rear of the bus and sat down.

It did not feel like a win.

***

One night, riding the funicolare in Napoli, my companion and I got off at the wrong stop. The area was seedy, even for Napoli, and there was palpable tension in the air.

Then an elderly woman approached us. "These streets no good for you!" she said. "These streets no good!"

I grabbed Elder Larson and hurried back to the funicolare.

The 8 pulled into the Mount Baker Transit Center and I stepped off. I'd hardly walked three feet when I felt someone grab my arm.

"This fell out of your bag," a young black man told me. He handed me a tiny plastic container sized to carry a boiled egg. I used it to carry my daily meds.

"Thanks." Looking into his eyes, I saw my future—an old man wandering away from his nursing home in the middle of the night and walking right in front of a bus.

***

Earbud day.

Train's "Play that Song" brought a smile to my face, kept hidden from the other passengers by my mask. I was wearing a new one, with the words, "If you can read this, you're now infected." Gail probably wouldn't like it, but I had rehearsed how I'd point out if she was close enough to be upset by it, she was breaking company COVID protocols.

Green Day performed "Boulevard of Broken Dreams," uplifting somehow despite the lyrics.

John Legend's "All of Me" was surely one of the best songs of the last ten years.

Maroon 5's "One More Night" felt hopeful, even though it wasn't.

I'd been planning to leave a not-for-any-special-occasion card on Brigham's desk last year, for him to find the morning of that fateful protest, just to tell him I loved him. I'd even selected one featuring the Northern Lights.

I had to go in to work early, though, in order to be able to join him on Capitol Hill later. So I'd decided to put it off until the following morning.

Leona Lewis sang "Bleeding Love," hauntingly beautiful. I hoped these artists who brought so much joy into the world enjoyed just a little of it themselves.

I saw flashing lights ahead and then a fire engine next to a tiny neighborhood park. One of the homeless tents had caught fire. Firefighters were putting out flames on some bushes separating the park from a brick residence.

A few homeless folks stood in front of their own tents, watching with expressionless faces.

***

"Oh, hey there," I said, nodding to the woman who'd joined me at the bus stop in front of the clinic, still keeping herself a safe distance away. "How's the knee?"

The woman cocked her head slightly, and then I saw recognition in her eyes. "It *is* Stage 1," she confirmed. "We're planning our approach and so far, so good."

"How's Andy's A1C?" Dagnabbit, I didn't even remember this woman's name. Had she told me and it didn't register because I was too focused on men? Why hadn't I asked for it?

She laughed. "I'm sitting now—it's not nearly as sexy—but we're keeping his A1C down around 6." She shook her head, laughing again. "You?"

"No consistent distractor yet, but I'm exercising more, and that's helping."

"Well, don't look at me!"

I chuckled. "No, no," I assured her. Then I took a chance on her sense of humor. "You lend Andy out to help fellow diabetics?"

"Oh my God," she said. "We've got to stop meeting like this!"

"My name's Todd," I told her.

"Megan."

We nodded at each other.

Then I looked down the street to check for the bus.

“All right,” she said. “I’ll ask Andy if he’s up for a Zoom call when we check his glucose.”

“What?” I choked out.

“We test first thing in the morning and again around 6:30 in the evening.” She pulled a slip of paper from her purse and jotted something down, handing it to me just as the bus arrived. “Call me,” she said.

We boarded, sitting several rows apart as we took off.

Chapter Eighteen: The Scenic Route

I could have walked to Skyway. It was almost certainly better exercise than the stationary bike, and the post office was only thirty-five minutes away by foot. Besides, the two hundred postcards I'd agreed to mail to voters in Virginia where a special election was about to take place didn't weigh much.

But there was a two-block section of the road without sidewalks, and with so many drivers looking at their phones, I couldn't risk it. So I waited for the 106 to head south.

A bowlegged Asian woman boarded two stops later.

And an obese white woman in her late twenties, maskless, boarded a stop after that. As she bumped into my seat on her way to the rear of the bus, I said, "Is wearing a mask really all that difficult?"

"I'm vaccinated!" she yelled, leaning over me.

So were 8000 patients in Germany who later discovered their anti-vax nurse had substituted their vaccine with saline. God only knew how much of that was happening in the U.S.

"I didn't ask if you were vaccinated," I said. "I asked if it was really all that difficult to wear a mask."

"Mind your own goddamn business!"

"My health *is* my business."

Every day there were reports of rude and confrontational passengers on airlines, but the crazy was everywhere. I'd had to ask a coughing woman at the grocery yesterday to put a mask on before I could check her out. She refused, I refused to wait on her, and my manager had to come over.

Missionary life taught me that much of life was hard. I just hadn't realized how many of the *easy* parts would be hard, too.

But knowing a conversation with anti-maskers was useless didn't really absolve me from trying, did it? A climate writer I followed, Mary Heglar, had tweeted the other day that we shouldn't worry about whether or not we were doomed by global warming. We should worry about what we stood for. And then stand for it.

Sturgis was holding another motorcycle rally in South Dakota. Over 700,000 people, almost all unmasked, unvaccinated, or both.

I'd seen a report about some COVID patients developing diabetes, that the virus somehow changed the function of cells in their pancreas so that they no longer secreted insulin but glucose instead.

I wondered if the virus was affecting our frontal lobes, too.

The woman continued to the back of the bus. I realized I'd made everyone else at least as uncomfortable as she had made them.

Something hit me on the head. I ducked instinctively and watched a plum bounce onto the seat beside me. I didn't turn around but could hear the maskless woman behind me giggling.

Just a few stops later, we reached Skyway and I pulled the cord. As I stepped off the bus, the maskless woman flashed her boobs at me through the window. It reminded me of the time years earlier when a mail carrier had discovered I was gay and tried to exorcise me.

When he'd finished casting out the evil spirit inside me, I'd sighed in relief. "Thank you *so* much!" I'd said, shaking his hand. "Now I can finally do it with a priest!"

***

The 11 was coming, but I really wanted the 8, so I shook my head to let the driver know he could skip this stop. Common courtesy, though not all drivers agreed. While most offered a short beep or a wave as they passed, I could see a few drivers, those as lax with their masks as the riders sitting behind them, throwing what looked like a sneer my way.

The 8 didn't arrive for another thirteen minutes. I climbed aboard and walked the length of the articulated bus, taking a seat across from the rear exit.

Two white men in their late twenties boarded a few stops later. One wore a T-shirt that read "6MWE." The other man's T-shirt featured a drawing of a hand, its thumb and index finger forming an "O" in the traditional "A-OK" sign which had in the last decade or so taken on a different meaning. The back of his shirt read, "I study Triggernometry."

If only the problem were with American racists. But I'd just finished viewing the Swedish series *Blue Eyes* a couple of nights earlier. The ending had been unsatisfying, to say the least.

A year or so after returning from my mission, I'd watched the movie *Greystoke*. Tarzan had been torn between life in London and his ape family in Africa. I'd been embarrassed to find myself identifying. I knew what it was like to be caught between worlds.

And the situation hadn't improved in the years since. I missed hamburger joints. I missed pizza bianca. I missed Gospel Doctrine class. I missed bathhouses. I missed CDs. I missed being partnered. I missed being single.

Well, *young* and single.

I understood when white people complained they were losing their culture. They *were*. That's what happened to culture. It changed and evolved. Gay culture had changed, too. No Grindr back in my day. You wanted sex? You asked for it in person. You wanted to watch a mainstream gay movie? They didn't exist.

Even now there weren't many. Independent gay movies, yes. Indie films and streaming channels like Netflix and Hulu had changed filmmaking for everyone.

Culture changed.

The bus stopped in front of the community center on 19th. An employee working the public showers had been struck by a homeless man last week. A white, middle-aged man, lean and with exceptionally unkempt hair, boarded now by the tennis and pickleball court across from the center. His lips were sunken, suggesting he might be missing teeth, his jaw covered with salt and pepper stubble. I could smell alcohol from four rows away.

The guy had almost certainly lost his driver's license or other ID in one of the many sweeps he'd endured over the years. Hard to get a job without an ID, even if he did manage to get sober.

Hard even to get assistance.

Hard to get sober even with a job and assistance.

But I saw he had a cell phone.

When I watched *Bulletproof Heart*, I realized that even if I could somehow afford to move back to Rome, the Eternal City I knew had changed so much I wouldn't fit in any longer.

The one benefit to growing old, apart from AARP, was perspective.

Society wasn't going back to pre-internet days. Folks weren't going back to landlines or snail mail. TV fans weren't going to settle for new episodes of *Father Knows Best*.

At sixty, I shouldn't be old enough to feel like I was eighty. But it was impossible to witness Seattle falling apart without feeling anger and despair and desperation.

Yet it wasn't the "Kids these days!" It was the adults, the ones in charge.

"Get off my bus!" the driver shouted. He was pointing at an elderly black woman dragging a torn garbage bag full of what looked like actual garbage up the front steps.

She spit in his direction before stepping back off.

The two young white men in T-shirts laughed.

But what else, I wondered, could the driver have done?

***

I tapped my card against the reader and started walking down the aisle, keeping an eye out for the best seat. The empty row over there was problematic because the woman in the following row was eating a corn dog. That other row across the aisle was one row behind the corndogger, but someone had left trash in the middle. A seat in the row behind that had something brown on it.

A man in his sixties beckoned me from the row behind the rear exit. I didn't recognize him, but with these masks, it wasn't always easy. I walked over, and as there were no empty rows back here, I sat when he patted the seat beside him.

"We've got to save the planet," he said the moment I rested my bag in my lap. "Everyone else is imploring it."

Mannaggia. He was one of those guys.

On PBS, I'd seen moose shot with dart guns stumble and collapse. Rhinos and elephants, too. With four score and seven extra pounds around my middle, I was my own anchor and looked like a falling moose in reverse when I tried to stand up. And with my lunch/water/phone/insulin bag on my lap as well, I was all but cemented to the seat.

"All these storms and droughts and fires," the man continued. "The disasters keep escapading."

I envisioned Janet Jackson on stage with Justin Timberlake.

Why couldn't she have pulled off his codpiece instead?

My seat mate might have been ill, but it wasn't as if he were wrong. A few days ago, it had rained for the first time in recorded history at the summit of Greenland.

I tried to look straight ahead, but the guy was leaning into my field of vision. His voice was a little slurred in addition to being muffled, and I realized I might simply be misunderstanding. Sometimes, when we made assumptions, we saw and heard what we expected.

I knew I should get up, but I didn't want to trigger him. Of course, avoiding a conversation while I sat beside him could be triggering as well. So might agreeing with him. Or saying anything at all.

Porca vacca.

"We can't address climate change with a blasé faire economy," the man said. "We've got to come together and make an asserted effort or we're doomed. *Doomed.*"

Now I knew how those poor souls felt on Piazza della Repubblica when we set up our streetboard next to the bus stop.

"Here," the man said, pushing a slim volume into my lap. "It's a copulation of essays I've written." Was he doing this on purpose? Even Archie Bunker hadn't been so consistent.

The book was too narrow to support any writing on the spine, the cover olive green, revealing the title and his name but no other image. I remembered reading the journal of a 17th century Italian rabbi who'd secretly spent household funds to self-publish a book, convinced the sacrifice was for the good of mankind.

Even if he couldn't tell his wife.

"Will you read it?"

I was the 8 sliding down Denny after the bridge iced over during a winter storm.

"Come to my place." The man patted my knee, but I sensed no gay vibes at all. Straight ones, either, for that matter. I'd only recently learned about asexuality. And if ever a man needed a dick in his mouth to keep him from talking…

"We'll have some toolong tea," he continued, "and I'll read to you."

Oh, come on. He *had* to be jerking me around. And what was it with everyone wanting to read to me? I felt like the old man in a nursing home whose family never visits but who the staff set up with strangers bringing yellow Labs for pet therapy.

Only I was an old man being sent to the homes of the volunteers instead.

The loneliness in the man's eyes was painful to witness. It felt dangerous to be so near it.

"Um..." I needed to get off at the next stop and take a later bus. Yet I couldn't simply reach across him for the cord. I'd need to excuse myself and walk away.

"We can sit outside if you feel more convertible," he said. "Please come." He stopped patting my knee and let his hand rest there. "It'll be safe, I promise."

The old man didn't *seem* like a serial killer.

"A man's home is his recluse," he continued.

John Speke in *Mountains of the Moon* shoved an awl into his ear to stop the sound of a beetle that had crawled inside. If the only voice in my seatmate's head was his own, that torture alone would drive him mad. And if he'd been doing this his whole life, I could only imagine how often he'd been bullied and beaten up as a kid.

Unless this was some kind of developing dementia. Perhaps he had a tumor. Or had suffered a stroke. I'd read enough Oliver Sacks to know the brain was a strange universe of its own.

How could someone who couldn't communicate even begin to ask for help?

"Please." He now looked about to cry. *Why* hadn't I pulled the cord sooner? I wanted Scotty to beam me up immediately. "Please accept my inclination. Please."

The man's hand was still on my knee. I placed my hand on top of his. "I'll call in sick today," I said. "Let's go sit on your porch and read some essays."

It was all I could do not to say "assays."

Chapter Nineteen: I'll Take the Low Road

"Hey. You awake?"

I blinked my eyes a few times and looked over at Anthony. He'd rung my doorbell at 3:00 a.m. and asked me to go for a ride now that he'd finished his calls for Logger. I'd slept through the ride, though, and had no idea where we were.

"Sorry," I said, my voice muffled by my mask. "I'm awful sleepy."

Anthony nodded. "I'm adaptable. Come on."

We were parked now, and I opened the car door. We were in front of Kubota Garden, just a few blocks from my house. During operating hours, Via vans waited at this neighborhood hub to bring riders to the light rail station or drop them off after picking them up on Henderson.

No Via were here at 3:00 in the morning.

"Don't shut the door," Anthony whispered. The apartments across the street were set way back, but there was no point advertising our presence with a slam. "Just lean over the seat."

I did, and Anthony walked up behind and started rubbing my ass. "I'm going to fall asleep again," I whispered back.

And I did, waking up when Anthony tugged my sweatpants down. I felt a dab of lube on my asshole, heard him unwrap a condom, and fell asleep again before he pushed his cock inside me. I woke up again for a few moments, vaguely hoping he wasn't stealthing but too sleepy to form a coherent thought or to reach back and check. He kept his rhythm so consistent that I fell asleep once more before he came.

Anthony helped me back into the car and drove me home. "You're a real pal," he said as I stumbled onto the sidewalk.

***

"I don't have to pay!" the black man shouted. "Drive the goddamn bus!" He slapped the plexiglass door protecting the driver and moved deeper into the bus, sitting in the first seat behind the disability section.

"Pay or get off," the driver repeated. He was white, young, probably no more than thirty.

"It's a pandemic," the passenger shouted back. "I don't have to pay. Drive!"

The driver picked up his handset and began talking into it. A couple of other passengers yelled at the offending rider, while others yelled at the driver. The passenger who'd refused to pay threw up an arm in the direction of the folks yelling at him. "Fuck you!"

I'd asked HR at the supermarket to provide training in de-escalation. People weren't just unruly at city council meetings. They were jerks in the soft drink aisle, too, worse now than ever.

But it hadn't been deemed an appropriate use of funds or time.

I could hear a siren in the distance slowly growing louder.

Per carità.

What could I say to convince the driver to call the police off? Or to encourage the rider to leave the bus? Even if I offered to pay his fare, I wasn't sure that would prevent what was about to happen.

I'd just seen a video on YouTube showing a right-wing pundit having a meltdown over the possibility the next James Bond would be portrayed by a black actor.

"They're replacing us! They're replacing us!"

And just the other day, a black woman who'd kept getting low appraisals on her home had asked a white friend to take her place during the next appraisal. She'd replaced her family photos in the house with pictures of white people. And the home had appraised at $100,000 higher than the highest of the other appraisals.

Police officers had dragged a black paraplegic driver from his car and thrown him onto the ground as he begged bystanders to "Call the *real* police!" to save him.

"Drive the bus!" the black passenger shouted again. He could hear the sirens, too, but he wasn't backing down.

And then the police showed up. Had they really needed sirens for something like this? The fare was only $2.75, and Metro offered discount fares for low-income riders who qualified.

A man's life for a bus fare.

What chance was there, after all, this guy was going to suddenly be all calm and cool and do what the officers told him? The asshole was going to get killed over two dollars and seventy-five cents.

And if I stood up and tried to intervene, I could be killed, too. Or at least arrested.

I didn't want to die for something so stupid.

But weren't almost all of these police killings over things just as ridiculous? Picking up trash in front of your own home. Riding a bicycle without a license plate. Forgetting to use your turn signal.

Even "suspiciously" driving the speed limit.

The first officer boarded the bus, and the driver pointed to the problem. Not that there'd have been any mistaking him. The black rider was giving the middle finger to the front of the bus.

Your life was supposed to flash before your eyes when you were facing imminent death. But what I saw instead was not being here when a miracle carbon capture technology was invented. And Palestine was being declared a sovereign country. When North Korea became a democracy. And the U.S. embraced Medicare for All. When scientists finally developed a vaccine against HIV.

"Come me with," the officer ordered the passenger.

"Fuck you!"

My heart was pounding so hard I thought I might have a heart attack. Why hadn't Dr. Kamdar ordered the damn lipid panel? He wanted to wait until next year.

Maybe I could fake a heart attack to distract the officers.

But an ambulance cost a thousand dollars. And my insurance didn't cover a penny of it.

Neither had Brigham's.

"Officer," I said, standing up. I was two rows behind the black guy. "Why don't I get off with this gentleman? I'll give him bus fare and stay with him while he boards the next bus."

These particular officers might behave perfectly, I realized. They might not need and certainly wouldn't appreciate my interference. But it was impossible to know until it was too late.

"Fuck you!" the man shouted at me.

"Come on," I said, moving toward the exit. "The next bus'll be along in just a few minutes. You can yell at me for butting in while we wait." I motioned again, and the driver, thank God, opened the rear doors.

The passenger's eyes darted back and forth between all the parties, and he seemed to reevaluate the situation. I motioned once more with a jerk of my head, and the man finally stood and followed me off the bus. I kept walking away and he followed.

When we were half a block down, I turned to him. "People suck," I said. "Life sucks. Let's go get a cup of coffee."

"Fuck you!" the man said, marching off down the street. At least he wasn't heading back for the bus stop. The bus was still there, after all, the officers and the driver apparently still conferring.

He hadn't even waited for me to give him money for the bus.

I understood enough to recognize the white savior complex. But I was just as familiar with the white not-my-problem complex.

The only thing worse than watching Brigham die would be to watch another senseless killing without making even the tiniest effort, no matter how ham-handed, to stop it.

I sniffed my armpits. I was going to stink all day at work.

***

Megan, Andy, and I decided that a Zoom glucose check wasn't going to work. After all, I could hardly watch Megan's distractive efforts while pricking my own fingers.

Her distractions were all about feel, not sight, and my proprioception wasn't strong enough to make the substitution.

But we went out to dinner in Columbia City tonight. Lots of outdoor seating, since a side street had been converted into a dining area. Andy turned out to be as outrageous as Megan. I was no match for their banter, but they were just as happy to perform as to engage, so we agreed to do this again "soon."

I knew how that went. Still, it had been a lovely evening. I walked past the old movie theater and ice cream parlor, crossed the street to stand in front of the bank, and eventually, a 7 pulled up.

"Hey, Todd," I heard a familiar voice call. "How's it hanging?"

"Hi, Tommy." I sat next to him, in the row with lots of leg room, the one right in front of the rear door. "How are you?"

"You have to answer my question first."

"Tommy…"

"Is it socially inappropriate?" he asked loudly, probably more oblivious than provocative. Before I could answer, he added, just as loudly, "Then I'll find out for myself." And he groped me.

Too bad I didn't have my glucose meter on me.

Chapter Twenty: Light at the End of the Tunnel

The forecast had promised a 30% chance of rain, but there was hardly a cloud in the sky.

Wildfire haze didn't count. On days like this, I wore my N95. A cloth mask wasn't going to cut it. And with the delta variant raging, I knew I should probably be double masking. But it was so hot.

A police captain somewhere in the south, an anti-vaxxer, had just died of COVID. He'd been taking a veterinary drug for deworming horses.

Parts of Tennessee had received 17 inches of rain in a few hours. Twenty people had been killed.

It wasn't really accurate to say "freak storm" anymore.

A popular evangelical preacher had promised that Jesus would fix everything at the Second Coming.

I was on the last leg of my commute. The 106 turned off of Rainier onto 51st. A Latina, maybe forty, tapped on the plexiglass shield protecting the driver and whispered something to him before returning to her seat.

The driver, a thin, black man with an eastern African look, pulled onto Renton and stopped in front of the convenience store, its Lotto sign flashing a seductive total. Then he stood and approached a woman huddled under a blanket in the first row behind the disability section.

"No smoking," he told her.

I didn't smell anything. I'd thought the woman was asleep.

The figure under the blanket moved.

"Get off the bus," the driver ordered.

The woman yanked off her blanket and grabbed her things, no small feat, as they included not only the blanket but a torn cloth bag and an overstuffed kitchen garbage bag. "Fuck you!" she shouted. "Fuck you…and you…and you and you and you!"

She was channeling Friedrich von Trapp.

The woman's hands weren't free for pointing, but she directed her glare at the other passengers nearby on her way out the back door.

Once outside, she put her things down and banged on the side of the bus. The driver returned to his seat and picked up his phone.

"Shut the door and go!" a man behind me shouted.

"Close the door before she gets back on!" another man yelled.

"Call it in later! We want to go home!"

The driver closed the back door and jerked the bus back into motion.

***

The elderly Asian woman sat in the bus shelter with her umbrella open, sweating heavily, the sun still beating down on her at an angle.

Several more undocumented immigrants had been found in the Arizona desert where they'd died of thirst.

Every day felt like the Day of the Dead.

I'd watched an old Steve McQueen movie last night to forget the world. Brigham and I had enjoyed singing stupid theme songs to each other.

The Blob.

Blondie.

Gilligan's Island.

I wondered if anyone thought of developing a sequel to the original *Blob*, which had ended by dropping the frozen but still very much alive blob on the Arctic ice. With global warming, the danger returns.

Of course, instead of an alien, or even an exciting movie about one, perhaps humanity would be facing additional pandemics as long-isolated pathogens emerged from melting glaciers and permafrost.

But at least MHz was coming out with a new Italian series set in Puglia. *Captain Maria*. I could hardly wait.

Another passenger walked up and stood by the sign. Almost forty but trying to look younger, he was white, muscular and rough looking, with "206" tattooed on his calf. Almost certainly a gang member.

***

Gail had been an extra-large pill today, a downright suppository that offered none of the usual joys of sphincter stimulation. First, there'd been a five-minute harangue about my stocking all the new spices in an area reserved for a different brand. It wasn't until she paused briefly at the 4:38 mark to snipe at another employee passing by that I was able to inform her Brett had been the one who did the restocking the day before. And he was off today.

Gail hadn't apologized but did agree to help me move the offending items to their correct location after she returned from lunch. Only she didn't return. She "remembered" a dental appointment.

So I'd been grumpy even before I missed my first bus on the commute home. The only free seat had been next to one with two orange needle caps lying on it. The second bus had broken down before I reached a decent transfer point, and then, when I did reach one, I still had to wait another twenty-five minutes to catch the last leg of the trip.

I'd left work an hour and forty-five minutes ago.

I gazed dully out the window as we passed an auto repair garage, a storefront offering interpretation services, and a tiny market advertising halal meat.

There'd been a clash in Portland the day before between white supremacists and anti-fascists. A man in a pickup truck threatened to blow up the Library of Congress in DC. A gunman had opened fire in a supermarket in Tennessee, killing one person and injuring over a dozen others. And a hospital in Mississippi overflowed with COVID patients.

In the plus column, my arms still had some scarring but no fresh scabs. The compression sleeves were working. And I'd lost another pound.

Well, eight tenths of a pound.

As we climbed up Waters, I caught a brief glimpse of the lake, a dark, flat expanse, the hills beyond it dotted with houses. Their lights promised life and love and connection.

Even if not for a crazy old man on the bus.

Almost at the end of the line, I was the only passenger left on the articulated vehicle. I still had plenty of company, of course. An empty soft drink can, a few crushed cheese curls, an empty sandwich bag smudged with grape jelly, and a green plastic comb revealing a single strand of wavy red hair.

I yanked on the cord for the Stop Requested sign, and two blocks later, the bus pulled to the curb. I waited by the back door, but it didn't open. I looked toward the front of the bus.

The driver waved for me to approach. "Can you exit out the front tonight, please?"

I started up the long aisle, not even sure who was driving. I didn't think it was the heavyset black man who didn't like me, or the grandfatherly white man who shouted a hello at everyone who boarded. The guy with the shaved head and longish white beard only drove during the morning.

Of course, it didn't really matter. I was far too tired to flirt.

As I neared the front, the driver opened the plexiglass door protecting his seat from the passengers, blocking the aisle in the process.

What the—?

Then he stood directly against the plexiglass and nodded a greeting. I turned to look behind me. Had I missed something?

"I've been watching you," he said.

The driver was in his late forties, judging by the minimum wrinkling on his forehead. He was white, with mostly brown hair that was graying at the temples. His slight paunch made me want to rest my head on his abdomen and listen to him gurgle.

"The first night I noticed you," he continued, "was when you made out with another guy in the back row."

Uh-oh. The Taliban in Afghanistan were luring gay men through social media and then either raping them or outright killing them as the U.S. prepared to leave.

Nobody was outside in my neighborhood at this time of evening.

There was a ravine just down the block.

Wait a minute. That smooch session with Tommy had been on a different route. Not that drivers always drove the same one every day. But—

The driver pressed his crotch against the plexiglass.

Maybe marketing *did* work. I was wearing my "Consenting Adult" shirt today.

I reached into my pocket, pulled out a tin of breath mints, then made a show of opening the tin and slipping a mint underneath my mask.

"I usually do my break at the bottom of the hill," the man continued, "but would you like to make out for a few minutes before you head home?"

Mannaggia.

"There's a camera on board." He motioned over his left shoulder. "Let's go out on the sidewalk." He took a step toward the door and swung the plexiglass shield against his seat, allowing me to follow him off the bus.

A large spruce tree blocked some of the light from the streetlamp, but when the driver pulled down his mask, I smiled underneath mine. His closely trimmed goatee gave his face added definition, necessary given his weak chin, but it was his lips that instantly won me over, curled up slightly at the corners in what seemed to be a permanent grin. The opposite genetic effect of what I'd seen in memes of Grumpy Cat on the internet.

I pulled my mask down, too. I had to generate my own smile, but despite the long day, it came easily.

"Nice face," the driver said. "Looks better when I'm not seeing it from forty feet away."

I laughed. "That's not a given, so thanks."

He offered his hand and I took it, letting him pull me to him. He didn't open his lips until they were almost on mine. His tongue must have had a frenulum made just for occasions like this because he was able to thrust it to the back of my mouth. I tried to be playful with my own tongue but was too absorbed in all the sensations he was creating with his.

A tickle here. A push there. Rubbing and swirling and more pressure. On the roof of my mouth. Against my tongue. It felt as if it were about to descend into my throat.

The sharp tang of musky cologne time-stamped the moment.

When the driver finally broke away, I felt more satisfied than if I'd cum.

"My name's Carson," he said. "I'm free on Wednesday." He reached over to caress my cheek. "Would you like to come over to my place for dinner?"

I tried to imagine what his tongue would taste like after a nice Indian meal or—magari—an Italian one. I pulled out my phone so we could exchange numbers.

Carson sent his first text before I reached my front porch. A photo. Of him sitting at the wheel of the bus I'd just left, with a knowing, teasing look in his eyes, and that adorable smile I couldn't wait to see again.

I still sucked on a chewable zinc tablet when I walked through the door.

***

Tuesday morning after boarding the 8 at Mount Baker, my phone pinged. I heard the sound so rarely it took me a minute to figure out what it was. I reached into my bag and read the screen.

"Would you like to get in my sling before dinner or after?"

Was Carson sexting me? Perhaps this qualified more as pre-sexting. "Is it just one or the other?" I texted back.

"You wanted during dinner, too?"

"LOL. It's always the quiet ones."

And in response to my "quiet" statement, the texting stopped. Had I offended him? One of the problems with the written word was the absence of auditory signals. Maybe—

The phone rang and I answered immediately. "Hi, Carson."

"I don't believe 'good' people are only allowed tame, polite sex," he said. "Or that only 'beautiful' people are allowed to enjoy each other's bodies." He paused to catch his breath, and I caught mine, too. "I hope we're on the same page."

"Uh, yes," I managed. "Uh-huh."

"Before you go to bed tonight," he continued, "I want you to text me three wild and crazy things you've always wanted to do."

"OK."

"We'll do one of them on each of our first three dates."

A planner and an organizer. "And when will we do the wild and crazy things on *your* list?" If anyone else on the bus was listening, they gave no indication.

"Oh, all right," Carson said, "if you insist. I know our first date isn't until tomorrow night, but I'll stop by your place after my shift this evening and we'll take care of the first one."

I laughed.

"You'll want to start drinking a lot of water around 8:00 tonight."

I remembered what I'd told Tommy, but somehow, my former reticence had broken free of its mooring, like a ferry during an autumn storm. I had no idea what I'd just gotten myself into, but whatever combination of hormones was circulating through my bloodstream right now, they sure made me feel alive.

Given the diabetes, though, I wouldn't start drinking any extra liquids until 9:30.

I got off the bus two stops early and walked the rest of the way to work. If there was one perk to riding public transportation, it was tailoring my commute when possible to squeeze in five extra minutes of exercise.

And enjoyable body or not, I could stand to lose a few more ounces.

***

Earbud day.

After that incredible night with Carson, I'd queued up only happy songs. While I understood infatuation and saw little value in it despite its tempting delights, it was impossible not to enjoy the ride.

Carson was nice. And fun. And that was enough. This didn't need to be "love."

But I couldn't deny that waking up at 2:00 a.m. as Carson penetrated me with a lubed finger didn't give me hope for the future.

Andy Grammer sang "Honey, I'm Good."

Charlie Puth promised he was only "One Call Away."

Pink's "Blow Me One Last Kiss" had me bouncing my head to the demand.

David Guetta showed he was strong as "Titanium."

I heard a noise and looked behind me. On the last row of the bus, someone was shooting up, despite the potholes.

Walk the Moon yelled "Shut Up and Dance."

Chapter Twenty-One: The Road to Recovery

The Taliban had taken over Afghanistan just days after the U.S. started withdrawing troops. A cargo plane had taken off with over 600 desperate refugees crowding into the hold. An Afghan footballer had been killed trying to hang onto the landing gear. Others desperate to leave fell to their deaths as planes took off. A suicide bomber murdered 170 people lined up hoping to escape theocracy.

As bad as things had been before, I could only imagine the fate of gay men there now. Or women. Or anyone at all not a religious fanatic.

Tommy boarded the bus at his usual stop and sat down beside me, putting his head on my shoulder. I reached over and squeezed his arm.

He squeezed my thigh in return and then sat up straight again. “Two customers yelled at me yesterday.” He almost yelled the word “yelled.”

“I’m sorry.”

“I told them they had to wear masks. Store policy.”

I didn’t even need him to elaborate.

"They called me a faggot." He said the word loudly, of course.

Over the past few weeks, some schools, and several entire towns, had started banning the Rainbow flag. A school board member in Florida had filed a criminal complaint against school officials for allowing a gay book in high school libraries. The board member also demanded that *The Hate U Give*, about a police shooting of an unarmed black teen, be removed.

Tommy had read another chapter of the dinosaur shifter novel to me the day before.

Some days, I was glad to be old.

"They called me a *faggot*!" Tommy repeated, even more loudly, as if unsure I'd heard.

I sighed, about to remind him of social propriety when he continued. "And *I* said, 'Faggots wear condoms! You guys like to breathe in everyone's face! It's like going to an orgy at an STD clinic!'"

Half the heads in the bus turned to look at us. You could only ignore reality just so long.

"But you're still going to work?" I asked. "Your boss didn't get mad at you?"

He turned to me, his face only inches from mine. "My boss wrote what I said and put it on a sign in the front window."

It didn't do to question his account too closely. However much of that story was true, I was touched that he'd told it. And while I rather liked when he rested his head on my shoulder, I couldn't think of anything else to do right then to show him how I felt but rest my head on his shoulder instead.

"There, there," he said. "It's going to be all right."

***

While I hated being invisible, sometimes it was worse being seen. Waiting at the transfer center, someone's eyes would fixate on my stomach and then slowly scan up to meet my eyes. Other times, after they'd stared at my belly in disgust, I could see them openly peering into my bag to see what kind of cakes and pies I'd packed for lunch.

Or at least I imagined that was their goal.

Whenever I ate a protein bar, I knew people thought I was eating a candy bar. If I snacked on protein chips, I knew they thought I was scarfing potato chips.

The only acceptable food for a fat person to consume in public was celery.

I'd cheated the first couple of years after my diabetes diagnosis, but I quickly realized there was simply no point. Corporations and government agencies could disguise their CO_2 emissions, but the Earth still had to deal with the real amount. The same was true of my body. Even if I could sneak in a snack when no one was looking, my body still had to process every extra carb or calorie. Sneaking didn't change reality.

Four stops in a row this morning, passengers weighing over three hundred pounds struggled their way onto the bus. I could feel the vehicle shake with each step they took. Blue soda pop in the hands of a teen across from me rippled like the puddle filling the T-rex footprint in *Jurassic Park*.

Some guy on YouTube—i.e., an unreliable source—suggested that the global rise of obesity and diabetes, even in developing countries, could be the result of an as yet undiscovered virus. Clicking around a bit more, I found another "expert" suggesting these health crises were the result of increasing levels of PFAs in the bloodstream of every human on the planet. Someone else thought it was because antibiotics and pesticides had killed too many of the good bacteria needed in our gut.

It wasn't unreasonable to distrust the government, or scientists hired by corporations, or the media.

But I still wanted a COVID booster the moment one became available.

***

I didn't notice the man wearing a black plastic garbage bag sitting in the seat just beyond the disability section until I sat in the row right behind him. Then, of course, I noticed.

He'd placed a torn piece of leather luggage on the seat next to him. In his lap, he used a *People* magazine as a tray. On top of the magazine, he'd poured some cereal into a used paper coffee cup, poured milk over it, and used the old coffee cup lid as a spoon.

When he accidentally spilled some milk onto the magazine, he growled like a bear and threw the magazine across the aisle onto an empty seat.

A young man wearing a yarmulke, with tzitzit hanging below his vest, boarded at the next stop. He almost sat in the *People*-covered seat but then veered away at the last moment.

On our fourteenth anniversary, Brigham had set a card on my desk addressed to "Rachel." When I'd opened it, I read, "Jacob worked fourteen years before he could marry Rachel. I've been lucky enough to have you this whole time. Just imagine what our 28th anniversary will be like!"

The man in the garbage bag poured cereal into his mouth directly from the box and then swigged some milk from the carton.

A middle-aged Filipina boarded the bus and sat in the disability section. She pulled something out of a bag and stared at it. A lottery ticket.

I remembered a scene from *Logan's Run*, contestants flying up into a tower trying to win their chance at living past thirty.

I'd loved the movie so much my mom offered to buy me a T-shirt. I'd wanted the one with Michael York as the Sandman but was too embarrassed to ask for it, so I got the one with Farrah Fawcett instead. And was too embarrassed to have anyone think I lusted after her, either.

I never wore the shirt.

***

I requested Saturday off at work, was granted the request, and then Gail called in sick and I was ordered in to cover for her.

I refused.

Instead, I caught the 60 to the Duwamish River Festival in South Park. I didn't really have the funds to contribute to the Native festival, and there wasn't much I could do personally to clean the toxic waste dumped in the aboriginal fishing site, but I could at least volunteer to help clean up the festival grounds itself after the party was over.

***

I waited at the SODO light rail station until Carson got off work and joined me from the bus yard across the street. He gave me a kiss and a bear hug.

"I see you have your overnight bag," he said.

"Condoms, lube, toothbrush, breath mints."

"Cock ring? Nipple ring?"

"And that toy you asked me to bring."

"Ah."

We'd be checking another item off our list tonight. And Carson had suggested that once a week we submit updated lists to each other, always keeping at least three new items there.

This time of night, light rail didn't run as often, but that gave us a good ten minutes to kiss while we waited. PDAs weren't public indecency. And we were outside where there was plenty of air circulation.

When we finally heard the train approaching, we pulled apart but then settled into the last row to hold hands during the next part of the trip.

"I saw an article about rural transit in South Korea," I said. I'd really become a convert while in Italy. Even our inferior public transit in the U.S. would be more effective if housing weren't deliberately zoned to keep it far from the stores residents needed to survive. My first few years back in the States, I'd fallen asleep to Claudio Baglioni almost every night, dreaming of moving permanently to Rome or Bologna or Milano or Torino or Genoa.

"Yeah?" Carson held my hand in his lap so I could tickle his cock through his pants with my little finger.

"Some counties subsidize cab rides for folks who live too far from bus routes."

While I wanted to live even closer to amenities than I did now, I also wanted to live in the woods, preferably near a lake I could jump into if the forest ever caught fire. But there was virtually no public transit in rural areas of America at all.

I remembered Cary Grant waiting at the bus stop by the cornfield.

"I see." Carson unlocked his fingers from mine and spread my hand across his crotch.

"Short rides are just nine cents each," I continued. "Longer rides only cost a little more."

I wanted to ask his perspective on zero-fare public transit, but he started to move my hand around on his crotch, and I took over the motion myself. Damn, he felt good.

The nearest other riders were several rows away, none of them looking in our direction. Carson leaned over and nuzzled his mask against my neck. This was *so* worth feeling sleepy all day tomorrow at the store.

The train stopped. "This is the train to Angle Lake," the pre-recorded voice announced as the doors opened.

"Only two more stops," I murmured, nuzzling against Carson's cheek in return. "I hope I can hold out till we reach your place."

"If you cum in your shorts," he whispered, poking his masked nose into my ear, "I'll sniff them while I'm fucking you."

"That wasn't on your list," I protested.

"It is now." He pulled down his mask and thrust his tongue into my ear.

"Fuck!" I tried to get as hard as I could, hoping to jizz while he tickled the grooves in my ear. If we were still dating by Christmas, I was absolutely demanding a professional nude portrait as my gift.

"You know," he whispered after our stop was announced a few minutes later, "you should apply for the

Public Transit Advisory Board." He pulled his mask back over his nose.

I didn't even know what that was.

"They have a vacancy right now." He placed my hand back on his crotch and slid two of his fingers underneath my balls and as far back along the seam in my pants as he could to press against my asshole. "An *opening*."

I creamed my boxer briefs with a groan. The purple ones.

Chapter Twenty-Two: Oh, the Places You'll Be Late To

I hoped no one called the police. I felt like a serial killer, wielding my pruning clippers while I walked the long way around the block to the bus stop. But so many of the neighbors refused to trim their heather and hemlock and holly. They neglected to cut back their blackberry vines and wintercreeper.

Lots of car owners never bothered to stroll through the neighborhoods where they lived.

Detouring into the street, maneuvering around parked cars, stepping over speed bumps, all while carrying two heavy bags of frozen bell peppers and veggie patties from the grocery wasn't fun. I could see annoyance on the mail carrier's face, too, as he tried to duck and dodge the protrusions along his route.

Mostly, I felt for the old man in his motorized wheelchair, walking his ancient dog slowly around the block, unable to escape the thorns and other obstructions. Once a month, I headed to work with my shears to open the path as much as I dared.

A machete might have worked better as I slashed my way around the block, but even a carving knife could get a guy shot, so I stuck with the clippers. Blackberry vines were the worst. I didn't want to throw them on the perpetrators' lawns, and I sure wasn't going to just drop them on the sidewalk. It would have been beyond rude to throw them onto the hoods of any cars parked along the curb. And it wasn't feasible to drag a huge yard waste bin to work with me on a leash.

Brigham had talked often of getting a dog, but I'd kept putting off a visit to the rescue shelter.

Last week, though, I'd finally broached the subject of "dog sitting" for the elderly man in the wheelchair if he ever needed help.

"My daughter will take him when the time comes," he'd said. But he'd thanked me before moving on.

I threw today's cuttings into the street along the curb, in front of and behind the cars parked there. While people would notice how annoying it was to drive over the briars and branches, they still wouldn't realize it was just as problematic to wade through it all in person.

Or in chair.

But I wasn't trying to teach anyone a lesson. I just wanted the old man and his dog to be able to get out of the house once in a while. After my last snips, I tossed the clippers in my bag and waited for the bus.

No Tommy today. Oh, well. I was anxious for my next chapter. But maybe I'd close my eyes instead and try to get in a little nap before work.

***

"Call," Carson told me, "but don't leave a message. If I don't answer, send a text."

"I don't understand."

"No one likes voice mail," he said. "There's always some important bit of information at the very end, and if you miss it, you have to listen to the whole damn message again. So much easier to read a text."

I nodded. Since I rarely received either texts or voice mail, I was usually happy with anything coming my way, but Carson did have a point.

"I'll text from now on." It was a relief to know he hadn't deliberately been rebuffing me. I paused, afraid to add the rest of what I was thinking. "I'm glad Brigham left messages, though. It's the only way I can still hear his voice."

Carson pulled me to him as the northbound train pulled into Stadium station. "I don't know *how* to check my messages," he whispered as a handful of passengers deboarded and a few others took their place. "I've pushed every button I can think of. I know I could look it up, but it's just not that important to me. Long messages *are* a pain in the butt." He rubbed his cheek against mine before pulling away.

"Thank you," I said, giving his hand a squeeze.

His brows furrowed.

"It's nice sometimes to feel like a woolly mammoth instead of a dinosaur."

***

"I looked forward to Medicare all my life," Brigham had once told me. "Then you turn 65 and find out it doesn't cover everything and you still can't afford to get sick."

We'd caught the 106 to MLK and transferred to light rail. The protest was at Westlake, where a year later we'd take part in our first BLM protest. I carried my sign high so that others on board could read it. "If Vision isn't part of health, then why are you disabled without it?" The back of my sign spread an easier message: "Universal Healthcare!"

Always more provocative, Brigham's sign read, "What do we want? Incremental progress! When do we want it? Over the next 30-50 years!"

Way, way too long, but it was impossible to convey a complex message in a pithy slogan. Still, he'd really tried on the other side of his sign.

"Debt-free freedom!"

"You were right," a white man said loudly to a woman sitting next to him on the train a few seats away from us. They were both around forty. "Seattle *does* have a bunch of old hippies." He thrust his middle finger in our direction.

"Hey!" I shouted across the car. "I was only seven when *The Mod Squad* aired!" I'd barely been baptized when the 5th Dimension sang "The Age of Aquarius."

My missionary companions and I had talked every day about Jesus ushering in a Millennium of peace soon, very soon, almost certainly by the year 2000.

Who knew that Jesus's betrayal would be worse than Judas Iscariot's?

"Nothing but lazy addicts!" the man hissed. The woman beside him laughed.

"I've never even smoked a reefer!" I shouted back.

Brigham had put his hand on my arm to calm me, but he spoke loudly when he said, "Now, sweetie, don't you remember that nice brownie I gave you on your last birthday?"

"What!?"

"I'm trying to get us both in a psilocybin trial if I can." When I frowned, he clarified. "Magic mushrooms. Microdosing's supposed to help with depression."

My mouth hung open for several seconds, and I forgot all about the obnoxious couple in the middle of the car. "Did you really give me pot?" I asked.

"*Legal* pot," he assured me.

I'd set my sign down and pulled Brigham to me, planting the biggest kiss we'd shared in years on his lips. He hadn't been able to maintain contact for long, but when we looked up, the tourists were gone.

"Maybe they'll warn their friends not to visit," a white woman two rows behind us announced. She waved her sign in our direction. "Christians for Expanded Medicare!"

***

An old Filipino man in a red silk shirt boarded the bus wearing a Power Rangers backpack. I watched out the window as a Latina threw a bag of garbage into a bin for donated clothing before boarding as well. She wasn't wearing a mask.

The bus had hardly started off again before she pulled the cord for the next stop. When the driver opened the doors two blocks later and no one exited, he sighed and continued on.

The woman pulled the cord again. At the next stop, someone else got off, but I could see the driver's eyes searching everyone in his rearview mirror. He closed the doors and drove on. Within two seconds, the woman pulled the cord again.

At the next stop, no one got off the bus.

The driver stood up, leaned against the plexiglass separating him from the riders, and said, "Where do you actually want to get off?"

"Downtown," the woman said, picking something out of her hair and throwing it on the floor. We were miles from downtown.

"Well, stop pulling the cord 'til we get there," he said. He sat down, but before he could pull away from the curb, the woman approached and threw her dirty sweater on top of the wheel well.

"You can't throw that there," the driver told her.

"You got a trash bag?" she asked.

"Throw it away when you get off the bus."

The woman stood and banged on the plexiglass. "I want off *now*!"

The driver seemed only too happy to comply. He sat down, pulled the plexiglass back to open the path to the front doors, and opened them. The woman grabbed her sweater, tossed it onto the sidewalk without exiting, and then sat back down.

The driver waited a moment longer, sighed, and drove on once more.

***

Clouds!

I set my bag on the sidewalk and opened my arms, luxuriating in the cool breeze. Middle of September and 58 degrees. Pure heaven.

A car pulled to the curb across the street, and two women in white shawls hurried over and into the church. The only singing I could make out was the low, deep chanting of the men.

A tiny drop of moisture brushed my hand, but I could see no other mist in the air.

A masked man in his thirties began walking up from the church door. I waved.

"Hello, Todd," he called out softly in his Ethiopian accent.

"Morning, Hosea."

When we'd first met at the bus stop several weeks earlier and he'd told me his name, it was all I could do not to tell him *my* name was also Hosea.

My first time through the temple, I was given a "new name." It was whispered to me along with a warning never to tell another living soul but to remember it always because it was the name I'd be called by during the Resurrection.

If I missed roll call, apparently, I was out of luck.

I'd gone through the temple that morning with a friend of mine, and after the ceremony, we met up again in the locker room. "Do you like your new name?" he'd asked.

"It's OK." I shrugged.

"I'm Hosea," he said glumly.

Another young man in his new Mormon underwear overheard us. "What?" he said. "I'm Hosea, too."

Then two other young men joined in. "Wait a minute! I'm Hosea!"

"No, *I'm* Hosea!"

I'd felt like Spartacus. I had no idea at the time that men were only assigned one of thirty-one names, depending on the day of the month.

The 106 appeared at the top of the hill and headed down. Hosea didn't hurry up the steep sidewalk, knowing I'd hold the doors for him.

He moved to the first row past the disabled section and waited for me to sit by the window before sitting beside me next to the aisle.

For the next twenty minutes, Hosea answered my questions about the archangel Michael. His voice muffled by the fabric and drowned out by the other noises surrounding us, his thick accent made it still more difficult for me to understand much.

Other than that he loved his religion.

Forty years after returning from Italy, I'd forgotten how that felt.

***

Perhaps it was the screaming baby that made me so irritable. Or the sun blazing through the train windows.

Maybe I was just a cranky old man.

COVID numbers had been rising steadily in Washington state, 2600 one day, 3200 a few days later, 3900 a couple of days after that, 4500.

"Hey, Typhoid Mary!" I called out to the middle-aged blonde coughing over and over and over while not wearing a mask. "Sounds like you've got a nasty cold there." Several heads swiveled in my direction.

"It's allergies, asshole!" Then she hacked some more.

"I didn't know people could be allergic to their own brains." The few people who'd resisted looking my way now succumbed to the temptation.

I could hardly think of a dumber thing to say to someone I was trapped inside an enclosed space with. But countless news clips showed that anger was contagious, and I wasn't immune.

I watched anti-maskers storm grocery stores in Los Angeles, ramming masked customers with grocery carts. I watched a right-wing politician who'd tested positive—and whose wife had just died of COVID—attend an anti-vax rally in Maine. I watched right-wing nurses in Mississippi turn pregnant women away who wanted the vaccine.

And I watched a reporter interview the mother of a nineteen-year-old woman who died of COVID after her family pressured her not to be vaccinated. "She kept calling for me, and I couldn't do anything."

"Stop harassing me!" the woman shouted. "Stop—" She couldn't finish her demand, breaking into another heavy bout of coughing.

No one had been sitting in the seats closest to her, but now those only two or three rows away gathered their belongings and moved farther away. A few of them headed down the narrow passageway leading to the other half of the car.

I hated when people made fun of the pastors and right-wing radio hosts who died of COVID, another every few days. I didn't want to make fun of this woman. I wanted to slap her. Not even slap some sense into her. Just slap her.

Violence was contagious, too. And we were all treating it with home remedies.

"Even if you've just got a cold or the flu," I said, "no one wants that, either."

Despite knowing I was 100% justified in calling this woman out, I still felt like a piece of shit. When the train stopped at Othello, I got off with several other riders and took a few deep breaths. Then I slowly walked over to Rainier to cool down, not easy in the blazing afternoon sunshine, and caught the 7 to Henderson.

The button for the crosswalk was broken, but when there was a momentary gap in the traffic, I ran across the street and waited six feet from a black teen with an auburn afro until the 106 arrived ten minutes later.

The black driver who opened the doors had his mask down around his chin.

Chapter Twenty-Three: Nothing Behind Me, Everything Ahead of Me

"Cazzo!"

I waved the driver of the 7 Prentice over—he was driving in the left lane, for God's sake—but he jerked his thumb over his shoulder at the 7 following close behind in the right lane. So the 7 Prentice didn't stop. The 7 stopped. But I didn't need the 7. I needed the 7 Prentice.

It was fair enough if two 106s were coming one right after the other for one driver to keep going and let the other stop. Those buses were traveling the same route.

But that wasn't the case with the 7 and the 7 Prentice.

And now it would take an extra twenty or thirty minutes to get home. Death by a thousand bus stops.

Porca la fucking miseria.

***

Almost two weeks had passed since I'd last seen Tommy. Three days in a row I'd tried to time my morning commute with his schedule, but he hadn't shown up at the bus stop. Today, I'd arrived early enough to catch the 7:01, skipped that one and the bus that came at our usual time, and waited for the next as well.

Still no Tommy.

I wondered if he was on vacation. Had he been fired? Had he quit?

I hoped he wasn't sick. Or his housemate. Maybe his work schedule had changed or he'd been transferred to a different job site, which affected his commute time.

I missed him reading to me on our way to Tukwila. Since we hadn't ridden together every day, we'd only made it through a third of the book.

So many regulars casually drifted out of our lives. Things would seem perfectly normal, and then three or four or five months later, I'd realize I couldn't even remember the last time we'd spoken.

What had happened to the mixed-race woman with two young children whose stroller I used to help secure?

Or the elderly Asian man who used to rub my belly at the bus stop in Skyway?

Or the stunning Hispanic woman I'd never spoken to whose Mayan nose was such a beautiful sight to behold every morning?

Most of these folks I'd never see again, and I'd never know why. I'd only know that I missed them.

***

A firm, muscular black man in his thirties boarded, wearing a neon yellow work hoodie with two silver reflecting stripes.

"Put on a mask!" the driver ordered.

The man staggered to the mask dispenser, pulled out a mask, and plopped down in the disability section. As the bus took off, he attempted again and again to put the mask on. First, he made a motion as if to hook one of the loops over his left ear but couldn't do it because his ear was inside the hoodie while the loop remained outside. Then he tried to slip the other loop over his right ear but faced the same difficulty. He couldn't seem to grasp the concept that the mask and his ears needed to be on the same side of the fabric.

The guy didn't seem drunk, though, or high. He struck me as sleepy, probably working three jobs.

***

"What do you want to be when you grow up?" Carson asked, holding my hand with both of his. We sat in the back row of the last car of the light rail. Though it was late, several other riders shared our car, so he didn't kiss or grope me tonight.

"When I'm 65, you mean?"

He smiled. Or at least I imagined he did. Carson's mask featured a dragon head while mine showed several offshore windmills. I'd finally bought a batch of five new masks, though I still wore the plain black one to work most days. That felt appropriate.

"You're the first guy who understood the question."

"How many times have you asked it?"

Carson chuckled. "Nothing gets past you."

Quite a lot did, really, but since it was in my best interest to have him think otherwise, I let him.

"I want to slide down a zip line in the Olympic rainforest," I said. "I want to spend a winter in a mountain cabin surrounded by snow. I want to star in a movie with a dozen old men having an orgy."

Carson nodded. "Same-ol', same-ol'?" he asked.

"Excuse me?"

"Well, next weekend I'm taking you to the rainforest," he stated matter-of-factly. "And the week after that I'll reserve a cabin up near Snoqualmie Pass."

"Really?" It was still late summer.

"Just for a weekend," he clarified. "Probably in January. That'll give you plenty of time to put in a vacation request at work."

"Are you pulling my leg?"

Carson glanced around quickly, putting his index finger to his lips, or where his lips would have been if they weren't covered by his mask. "Not 'til we get back to my place," he whispered. "Show some constraint."

"And the orgy?" I asked, not quite as loudly as Tommy might have, but loud enough to generate a genuine look of surprise in Carson's eyes.

After staring for a moment, he shook his head. "I may have met my match," he said. "Doesn't happen often."

"How many times have you tried?"

He clapped loudly, drawing attention from several other riders that my orgy comment hadn't. "OK," he said. "For that, you get dildoed twice tonight before I fuck you so you're good and sore before I start."

"What makes you think I'm not used to three cocks up my ass in one night?"

God only knew what the other riders were thinking, if they were even paying attention to us any longer.

Carson pulled his mask down and stuck out his tongue. And I simply couldn't help myself. I pulled him to me to take full advantage of his offer, presenting him my ear in return.

***

I was a little embarrassed, and embarrassed about feeling embarrassed. But I held my sign high while I waited for the bus. The whole point of participating in the rally, after all, was to get an essential point across.

It wasn't "to raise awareness." Everyone knew homelessness was a problem. The question was what to do about it.

A driver honked as she passed by.

The thing about honks is they could either mean "Yay!" or "Fuck you!"

"It won't trickle down," the first side of my sign read. "They'll build spaceships with it."

When no one else honked over the next couple of minutes, I was afraid the message was too long, so I flipped the opposite side toward oncoming traffic.

"Housing First!"

It had worked in Finland and almost everywhere else it had been tried.

I missed Brigham.

As the bus approached a moment later, the driver didn't seem to be slowing down. Sometimes, when they were distracted, drivers accidentally missed stops. Every once in a while, it felt more deliberate.

Was it my sign?

I waved it to catch the driver's attention, feeling like the old, crazy guy on Broadway who used to wear a sandwich board in front of the gay bars. "Repent! The end of the world is near!"

The bus slowed down quickly and pulled over. "Sorry," the driver said as he opened the doors. "Arguing with a guy about masks." He nodded toward the cabin.

I thanked him and climbed aboard, sitting in the first seat past the disability section so everyone behind me could read my sign while I continued to the rally on Capitol Hill.

Several stops later, another protester boarded. The front of her sign read, "Other poor people aren't the reason you're poor." I gave her a nod and turned to read the back of her sign as she passed by.

"Tax the rich!"

I didn't feel embarrassed anymore.

Except for the embarrassment I felt for needing validation not to feel embarrassed.

***

I tapped my card on the reader and glanced up at the clock showing four minutes and fifty-two seconds had passed since the last light rail headed north. I strolled down the platform until I reached the Evolution of Man to wait for the next train. Meeting Carson at Stadium station was becoming quite the event, twice a week now for almost three weeks.

Casual and comfortable.

This time of night, there weren't many people waiting for the train, and I was able to find a seat in the first row past the doors. A couple of black tourists, masked, sat with their suitcases in the middle of the car, talking about France withdrawing its ambassador to the U.S.

Two white tourists, also masked, chatted happily about the former national security advisor calling for America to have only one religion—theirs.

Just after the train left Othello, my phone pinged. Some pre-sexting from Carson to generate some pre-cum?

"Gotta cancel tonite. Sorry. Something came up."

I'd watched *The Brady Bunch* enough as a kid to remember Marcia's strategy to get out of a date. "Have a good time," I texted back. I almost meant it. Carson had every right to make the best decisions for himself. We weren't in a committed relationship, after all.

But that didn't erase the need for manners. I'd already told Anthony not to stop by anymore. I was perfectly capable of feeling horny without also feeling desperate.

Or so I kept telling myself.

I got off the train at Columbia City, crossed to the other platform, and ten minutes later caught a train heading south. Three Asian guys in their early twenties, all maskless, boarded at Othello, laughing at everything they said to each other, tiny airborne droplets floating throughout the car.

A right-wing doctor in Idaho had just called vaccine mandates "needle rape." Tourists from Texas had attacked a restaurant hostess in New York who asked for proof of vaccination before she would seat the group indoors. A couple in Texas who went to a restaurant in their own town were kicked out *because* they wore masks.

Over 692,000 Americans had died of COVID so far. And that was almost certainly an undercount.

739,000 Americans had died of AIDS since its first reported cases in 1980.

I was so very tired.

How many times could one run the gauntlet without suffering a fatal blow?

Chapter Twenty-Four: An Unscheduled Stop

I was thinking about what to say or not say to Carson about last night and only gradually noticed a man looking at me from across the car, probably twelve or thirteen feet away. I thought he might have boarded at Beacon Hill. The guy was about fifty and slender, with light brown hair mingled with a few gray strands. He wore a black running suit, clearly not on his way to work even though we were heading downtown.

I turned my head to glance into the rows behind me. When I looked back at him, his eyes were clearly locked on mine, definitely cruising. I almost laughed at the absurdity. Even in my prime, this would have been a hard guy to reel in.

Public cruising was always problematic because it had to be at least reasonably subtle. Was he looking at me because I was enormous? Had I been staring at him without realizing it? Did I remind him of someone? Was he nervous? Was he into me? Maybe *he* was lost in thought about something and not even seeing me. Perhaps I was imagining the whole thing.

Since there was no way to know, I simply cruised back. A few stops later, the man walked across the car to sit in the seat directly opposite me. A good sign but still problematic. I could no longer casually look in his direction. Now I'd have to physically turn and look across the aisle. It would be clear he was the object of my attention.

The jogger positioned one hand so that it "almost" looked like he was fondling himself, but it was hard to be sure. I stole a more direct glance. When our eyes met, we both looked away. Then I turned back and held his gaze the next time our eyes met. He did the same.

But we still couldn't be too obvious, so we both looked away yet again. The next time I glanced over, he "scratched" his crotch, not looking at me until he finished but keeping his hand in his lap. I moved my left hand to rest on my crotch but didn't make any other suggestive moves.

What if we ended up chatting? I couldn't tell him I was on my way to the clinic on Capitol Hill for an HIV checkup. That would be a real weenie shrinker.

I hoped he was getting off at my stop or would at least follow me if that wasn't his real destination. But he stood up after University Street to deboard at Westlake.

Damn.

I didn't want to miss my appointment, but opportunities like this were too rare to squander. I stood up about ten seconds after he did and prepared to deboard at Westlake, too.

The guy cruised me openly, alternating eye contact with looking at our reflection in the glass. In my head, I was always "me." I felt the sexual energy in my brain, in my soul, and could sometimes forget how huge I was, at least briefly. Following the jogger's gaze, I was horrified anew at my enormous image in the window. But the guy still seemed into me, for whatever reason, and I was determined to see this through. The brain was our most important sex organ, after all. I had that, willing body parts, and the attitude necessary to take advantage of every resource.

When the jogger stepped off the train, he headed straight for the elevator, and I followed him inside. He pushed the button, the doors closed, and then, without wasting another second, he reached for my crotch and I reached back for his. I was surprised to realize I was already hard, even without a preemptive dick pill, a bit surprised that the other guy, despite his aggressively sexual behavior, was completely flaccid.

We fondled each other without reaching past cloth barriers as the elevator rose to the mezzanine. The man moved closer and brushed his masked cheek against mine. That felt even better than the groping. But when we stepped off the elevator, reality set in.

"I'm afraid I have an appointment," I said. "I need to get back on the train. I just wanted a chance to talk and exchange numbers."

"I have to be discreet."

"That's cool."

"You have a card?"

Oh my God. Why didn't I have a card? The one slip of paper with my name and number on it I'd given to Rocio. Why in the world hadn't I replaced it? What was wrong with me?

I scrambled to tear off a piece of paper from notes I'd prepared for my doctor, but then I couldn't remember my phone number. It wasn't as if I called myself or gave it out very often. I pulled out my phone to look up my number so I could scribble it down.

Whatever sexual energy had been in the air was quickly dissipating.

I handed him the paper. He took it without a word and walked off while I headed back down the stairs to the platform and waited for the next train.

I was *not* going to see this as a failure, I told myself, no matter how obvious the man was never going to call. This was a success. Someone had flirted with me, we'd had a bit of fun in the elevator, and if that's all it was, that was OK. A few guys were paying *some* attention to me. I was going to take the win.

***

I didn't ride the streetcar often, the line on Capitol Hill the only one even close enough to bother with. That streetcar ran in the same lane as regular traffic and so was no faster or easier than a bus. If anything, it was worse because if it broke down, no other tram could use those tracks any longer.

I'd spent a couple of hours with Megan and Andy at the Frye. She used a cane because of her treatments but seemed in good spirits.

"Would you have a three-way with her?" she asked Andy a couple of times, pointing to different portraits in the main gallery. "Or him?" He rolled his eyes while she winked at me.

I almost made a joke about the South Lake Union Trolley—the SLUT as we called it locally—but caught myself. Why did a woman's sexual enthusiasm make her a slut while a man's made him fun to be with?

This morning when I'd told Carson my plans for the day, he'd started singing. "Bang! Bang! Bang! On the trolley!" thrusting his hips forward with each bang.

Sometimes, sexual enthusiasm was annoying.

On Jackson, I stepped off the streetcar and crossed to the sidewalk to wait for either the 106 or 7, whichever came first. Several masked grocers came out of an Asian grocery on the corner with ingredients for their dinners. Three black men spread a blanket on the sidewalk a few feet down to sell suitcases.

There'd been a shooting on this corner last week.

An elderly Asian woman sitting on the bus bench gave a tongue lashing to an elderly Asian man who stared dully at the pigeons pecking along the curb. A young Asian girl zipped by on her skateboard.

I felt more fragmented every day, happy one moment, angry the next, apathetic the moment after that. I could witness abject poverty day after day without being fazed. One day, I'd hear about Texas being devastated by a major freeze. Another day I'd see drought in Kenya, flooding in Pakistan. The next, I'd watch a fuel tanker explode in Sierra Leone and kill ninety people. All that just this year alone. And life trudged on.

Or didn't, depending on where or who or what you were.

I saw a bus straining its way up the hill from the International District and squinted.

It was the 7 Prentice! "Yay!" I was still Charlie Brown, even after all the Lucys.

***

Another maskless wonder on light rail. The blonde tourist, with her mask below her nose, spoke to another blonde, appropriately masked. They blocked the aisle with their roller suitcases.

"Ma'am?" I said, waving from my seat on the other side of the doors. *"Ma'am!"* I waved again.

The women looked in my direction. I raised a roll of blue athletic tape in the air. "Do you need some help keeping your mask up?"

The woman's jaw dropped. She blinked a few times and then thrust a finger toward me. "Who the hell do you think you are?"

"Someone who wants to live," I told her. "You've had a year and a half to find a mask that fits. Figure it out."

"Well, you keep talking like that," she spat, literally—I could see droplets flying from her lips—"and someone's going to kill you."

I envisioned the entire scene as a viral video that ended up getting me fired but was too tired to care.

"We had 900 new COVID cases in King County yesterday," I said. "Could you please pull your mask up over your nose?"

I kept my eyes locked on hers, so I wasn't sure how other passengers were reacting. Not well, I expected. Given the daily numbers, people seemed better at avoiding emotional discomfort than the virus.

"Stop causing trouble!" her friend ordered me.

"Why are you escalating this?" the first blonde demanded.

Because my workplace refused to train me, I almost told her. "Ma'am," I said, "you're the one with a gun pointed at me."

"I don't have a gun!"

At this, I heard rustling and could see movement all around us. People were heading toward the narrow passage leading to the other half of the car.

"You have two barrels pointed at me. Pull your goddamned mask over your nose."

Out of nowhere, the lyrics to "Another Day in Paradise" started drifting through my head.

I wondered if I was developing dementia.

Then I wondered if I'd wondered that before.

***

My day off. It was utterly ridiculous to even consider leaving the house. But what if?

What *if* in my hurry the day I'd met the jogger I'd written the wrong phone number down? My glasses had been awful foggy. The logical part of my brain told me the guy wasn't interested, hadn't even been particularly interested the day we'd flirted but had pursued me because I was all that seemed available at the moment. Other moments had come since and there was no need for him to go out of his way and relive what was at best a moment of horny, pragmatic "make do with what's on hand."

When I'd gotten home that day, I'd gone online and finally put up my own ad, completely honest about my stats, specifying what I liked and didn't like, ending with an offer to keep an open mind if someone wanted to suggest something not on the list.

No one had responded the first day. I'd reposted the ad the next day and again no one responded. No one. Not a single person.

But *maybe* if I ran into the jogger again, *he'd* still be willing to make do.

Losing had to be better than giving up.

It was pathetic accepting my status as the object someone reluctantly settled for. I knew it as I boarded the 106. I knew it as I waited at the Rainier Beach station.

And waited. And waited. Trains were supposed to run every eight minutes, and when I arrived, the clock showed seven minutes and thirty-four seconds had already passed since the previous train had left. Then the clock read 10:22. And 13:51. And 15:49.

Something had happened. But the tracks were all above ground to our south. Clearly, the train hadn't hit a car or pedestrian.

So what *had* happened?

Finally, at 16:36, the northbound light rail pulled into the station. It was crowded, and two dozen riders rushed to grab the few remaining seats. I'd waited at "the spot" for the front entrance of the appropriate car and was first in line, heading for the same seat where the jogger had cruised me a few days earlier.

The two seats across from me had been roped off with yellow caution tape. On the seats and the floor in front of them were a handful of blue surgical masks, several with something brown on them.

A coffee spill?

The row directly behind those seats was empty, with several more paper masks on the floor, several of them also stained.

That wasn't coffee.

During the delay of eight minutes, something frightful must have happened, and yet the car was still full of people. No one acted as if anything were amiss.

We all had someplace to be, I supposed.

I was still ahead of schedule and planned to sit on a bench at the Beacon Hill station until ten minutes past the time the jogger must have boarded the train where we'd met originally. I absentmindedly tapped my glucose sensor. My numbers had been quite good lately, below 100 most of the time.

I hadn't done any finger sticks to verify the readings, of course. Like Fox Mulder, I wanted to believe.

Halfway to Othello, the train stopped and the conductor made an announcement. "We are aware of the biohazard aboard the train. We'll be stopping at Beacon Hill, and everyone will need to deboard and take the train directly behind us."

The other riders barely looked up from their phones. Did no one else find this odd? There was a biohazard but we were going to keep everyone on board for *four more stops*? The conductor would have to open the doors at each of those stops to let people off who'd reached their destination, and there'd be no way to keep folks waiting on the platform from boarding.

But whatever. I was heading to Beacon Hill anyway. I'd stay on board. I was already sitting right across from the contaminated masks. I did wonder, though, what riders in the other cars thought when they heard "biohazard."

Had terrorists had sprayed anthrax into the air? Ricin? Why weren't they all beating on the doors to escape?

Many of the riders did get off at Othello. And more got off at Columbia City and Mount Baker. But a few other riders boarded at each stop, too. As soon as the doors closed each time, the conductor repeated his announcement.

Finally, when the doors opened in the tunnel at Beacon Hill, everyone walked off the train. I found a bench and sat down to wait, still forty-five minutes early for the train I was hoping the jogger would board. I felt a bit stalkerish, of course, and thought perhaps I should just head back home before I embarrassed myself.

Bang! Bang! Bang! Bang!

What the hell was that?

Probably two hundred people stood on the platform waiting for the contaminated train to leave so the train they'd be allowed to board could pull into the station. But our train wouldn't move.

Bang! Bang! Bang! Bang!

People yawned, looked at their phones, bit off a piece of their croissants or sipped their coffee. I stood and looked into the train. In the second half of the car I'd been on, three transit security officers looked at the floor in front of the disability bench. They chatted calmly, pointed, discussed, and chatted some more.

Then a female officer hit the partition beside the disability bench. Bang! Bang! Bang! Bang!

Someone must be on the floor.

Was the biohazard an actual person?

Two of the guards kicked gently at something. One of them tried to pick it up. The other guard banged on the partition again.

And finally, a young black teen sat up sleepily. The security officers talked to him, tried to get him to stand, and finally spoke into a handset. The doors closed and the train slowly pulled out of the station with the three officers and the teen still aboard.

I sat back down on the bench. It was divided into three sections, with sharp ridges at equal intervals to prevent anyone from lying down. Some kind of protective coating had peeled away in a dozen areas.

One minute later, another northbound train pulled up, and almost everyone boarded. Two minutes after that, the next train pulled up and most of the remaining riders climbed on. But not everyone. A few were still hoping for a less crowded train.

And then I saw him. The jogger wasn't "due" here for another forty minutes. The window of uncertainty was the whole reason I'd come so early, and I found myself shocked it had paid off. The man in his black running suit looked about with a slight air of confusion, almost certainly wondering why everyone hadn't boarded the train he'd just missed.

I felt way too stupid to approach him. He'd *know* I was an idiot.

But if he never spoke to me again, how was that any worse than his never speaking to me again?

I stood up and walked over. He briefly glanced my way but then turned to look back onto the tracks for the next train. I could see the moment he froze when it dawned on him who I was. He turned back around.

"Fancy meeting you here."

"Just followed the pheromones," I said.

He laughed. Thank goodness. Then he motioned to the other riders. "What's going on?"

"There was a biohazard on an earlier train." I explained the past several minutes, trying to avoid the most repulsive details.

The man shook his head. I could imagine him losing all interest in a sexual encounter after that. Or feeling ashamed that public transportation was a place he sought other men.

"What I just saw was pretty disgusting," I admitted, "but I'd still be up for exposing myself to some of *your* biohazardous material."

The man looked at me for a long moment before replying. "Be still my heart." He offered his elbow and I tapped mine against it. "My name's Samuel."

Chapter Twenty-Five: The Road to Success

Carson wasn't on duty, but he still had access to the comfort station at the transit center, even if the routes he drove didn't stop here. When I nodded toward it, he shook his head. "Let's save it for the trail."

The moment Carson had suggested the outing, I'd ordered a cell phone booster, afraid I might not get a signal on the mountain. And I wanted to take some pictures.

"We'll go off the main path."

Fortunately, GPS worked even with no cell service. To be honest, though, my biggest fear was being caught in an unexpected wildfire. Things hadn't been as bad as expected here in Washington state, but down in California, firefighters were wrapping the bases of giant sequoias with fire-resistant blankets as fires swept toward a grove of the huge, ancient trees.

"It's warm," Carson went on. "We won't freeze to death. We've got plenty of water. And we both have extra fat to burn."

But I hardly needed convincing, already excited to snap a few 'couples' selfies, even if the relationship only lasted another three weeks. *Carpe foto.*

It was important to remember the good times.

"You're not the first guy I've fucked in the woods," he added. "I know a place."

"OK, Petula. I trust you."

"You don't yet," he said, giving my shoulder a squeeze. "But you will in time."

Considering the things we'd already done in private, that trust was growing pretty fast. But the reality was we still barely knew each other. He'd never be Brigham, and I'd never be…who would I never be? I didn't even know.

I hoped the bus would come soon. A real outing seemed to elevate the relationship.

To "significant" casual sex.

A middle-aged white woman, almost skeletal, slowly pushed a grocery cart toward a dumpster across the street. She struggled a moment to lift the lid and then transferred two small bags of garbage from her cart to the dumpster.

"You go hiking much with your husband?" I asked.

"Which one?"

I laughed. "How many have you had?"

Carson shrugged. "Three so far. But I'm anticipating a fourth before too long."

I didn't know whether I should feel a thrill or roll my eyes.

I felt a thrill.

"The first died of AIDS back in the nineties." Carson had already told me he was positive on our first date. He'd been relieved to learn I was, too. "The second left me for a nun." He looked directly into my eyes. "I'm not kidding. We'd been together almost ten years by that point." He lifted both hands in supplication. "But the heart wants what the heart wants."

"I suppose."

We were silent a few moments. I checked the sign for the shuttle out to the hiking trails, though I knew perfectly well the bus wasn't due for another ten minutes. A thin, black man, probably only thirty, shuffled past, wrapped in a dirty blanket. A white man, older, stood several yards away, pissing against the back of the bus shelter along Rainier.

"And the last guy?" I asked.

"I was hoping you'd be distracted by the nun."

"Counting to three is pretty easy."

"You'd think, wouldn't you?" he said. "But Jathien kept acting as if three was the same as two. That five and six were the same, too."

"I see."

"Were you and Brigham monogamous?"

This was one of those dealbreaker conversations. I wished we were having it at the end of the day, not the beginning. I'd seen Samuel again and hoped to keep seeing him on an ongoing if irregular basis. "For the first ten years," I said. I paused to gauge his reaction but because of the mask, I could only see part of his face, and he managed to keep a straight forehead.

"And then?"

"Then he wanted to play a little." Now it was my turn to shrug. "By that point, I was, too. Given our background, we had to at least consider polyamory."

"And what did you decide?"

A fire engine from the station two blocks away started blaring its siren.

"We were open to it," I said. "Just never found the right guy."

Carson nodded. "You hadn't met me yet."

An 8 pulled up, and I almost boarded out of habit, stopping when Carson tugged on the back of my belt. A young Asian man in his twenties and a black woman in her forties stepped on.

"So we played once in a while," I said. "Sometimes together, sometimes not. I found I wasn't jealous. I just wanted Brigham to have a good time. And…"

"Yes?"

I shrugged again. "As I got heavier, he didn't enjoy me as much as he had earlier."

"How odd," Carson said. "I'm finding you absolutely delightful in bed."

"Well, we've only been in bed twice," I pointed out.

"So you're not counting the sling? Or the balcony? Or the—"

"Brigham and I weren't quite as adventurous together," I said. "And I hadn't yet discovered sildenafil, which makes a difference."

He raised an eyebrow. "You discovered that *after* he died?"

"A hard dick's not just handy when you're with another guy. It's also useful when you're in the shower."

Carson moved behind me and started rubbing my shoulders. I'd really be fine with a sexual friend. But I had to admit, the possibility of having an emotionally intimate relationship again made me almost hopeful.

I kept seeing the framed sign in my kitchen nook.

Two other hikers had gathered near the bus stop, easy to spot because of their gear. The best part of this route was that it wasn't mostly poor people who rode.

A truly developed country, I remembered telling Brigham, wouldn't be one where more poor people owned cars. It would be one where rich people rode public transportation, too.

I reached over and held Carson's hand.

As the shuttle approached a few minutes later, Carson leaned forward and whispered in my ear. "You should know I brought enough lube in case we're lost for a week."

I groaned. I was *not* in the mood to be discreet. And now he'd just triggered an additional release of hormones, which were already flowing at a pretty high concentration. "You fucker." I punched him lightly in the stomach.

"That's the idea."

***

The only safe spot on the train seemed to be the area reserved to hang bikes, so I stood in the cubbyhole and held on.

When my phone pinged, I tried to read the screen. It was especially hot and humid today—"sultry," as Anne Ramsey would say—so my glasses kept fogging. "Had incident in flight," Kevin wrote. "Woman waving flashlite. Said if you're vaxxed you'll glow with black lite. But no spitting today. A win."

Kevin and I used to teach Catholics in Rome that Native Americans were descended from Jews.

"Is it better to be on this side of the crazy now?" I texted back.

"You bet."

But I wasn't sure. When you believed, you were always convinced that eventually you'd come out on top.

***

The driver had just closed the front doors when I saw a young woman come running around the corner carrying three bags of groceries. One bag was paper, torn, with produce hanging out the bottom. The driver saw her, too, and opened up just as the woman started slapping at the doors.

"Thank you, thank you, thank you!" the young woman said, jogging up the steps and then lumbering down the aisle, her bags hitting a passenger seated in the disability section. Then she plopped down in the first row past that, right in front of me.

"Oh yeah, oh yeah, oh yeah," she said. "Thank you, thank you, thank you!" The woman might have been Latina but spoke with a standard American accent. Her hair was cropped close, her face covered with acne. And she wore her mask under her chin. "Whoo boy! Whoo boy! Whoo boy!"

The man in the disability section stood up and walked to the back as the bus took off.

"Fuck!" the woman suddenly shouted into the air. "You can't even buy a fucking bottle of water! Fuck! And you aren't even disabled! That's what *really* irks me." She slapped the top of the dividing wall in front of her. "It irks me! It irks me!"

I grabbed my bag and moved across the aisle, thinking about Ricardo Montalbán in *The Wrath of Khan.*

The woman continued like this for several more stops. She was probably heading downtown, past Westlake, so we'd be sharing the bus until I got off. When we started through Capitol Hill, the woman shouted as if she'd seen a ghost. "Oooooh!"

I noticed a delivery truck parked on a side street, employees carrying boxes of food to a small grocery.

"Look at the bodies!" the woman shouted. "Oh my God! The bodies! The bodies!"

Now I thought about Genevieve Bujold in *Coma*.

Someone yanked on the cord, the Stop Requested bell dinged, and a moment later, we pulled over to the curb. A young white man exited through the rear. "Thank you, Driver," he called as he stepped out of the bus.

The driver waved a weary acknowledgment into his rearview mirror and drove on.

Chapter Twenty-Six: Take Only Memories, Leave Only Footprints

"Don't you ever want to have sex in the freezer at work?" Carson nibbled my ear in the back row of the southbound train.

"Not really," I said.

"How about in the manager's office?" he suggested, kissing my neck. "Or the break room?" He trailed his index finger from my knee to my crotch. "Or the employee bathroom?"

To be honest, none of that had ever occurred to me. The only "exotic" sex I'd had was while looking for an apartment on Capitol Hill many years earlier when the landlord had wanted to illustrate how roomy the shower was.

He'd made unannounced visits in the middle of the night every few months "just to make sure everything's OK." I realized even at the time his behavior was inappropriate if not illegal, but I'd enjoyed his company and never turned him away, more disappointed than he when I finally decided to find a larger place.

"No," I said, "I've never had sex at work."

Carson lightly pinched one of my nipples. "You didn't answer my question," he pointed out before thrusting his tongue down my throat. Only one other person sat in our car, a young white man, masked, with dark hair shaved off one side of his scalp, and a tattoo I couldn't make out on his neck. He ignored us completely.

Carson's tongue seemed to be inflatable, filling my mouth entirely once inside, the way a perfect cock up my ass made me feel satiated rather than stuffed. He slowly withdrew, the tip of his tongue still touching mine even as he pulled away.

"I've never worked anywhere interesting enough to want to have sex there," I elaborated.

"Ah." Carson kissed me again until the train pulled into the next station. We sat looking out the window for a few moments, holding hands, his little finger tickling my palm. "There's a comfort station at the transit center for the route I'm driving tomorrow," he said. "I know you'll be pretty sore by then—"

"Excuse me?"

"—if things go well tonight. But I'm going to bring you to work with me in the morning and fuck you one more time before we part ways for the day."

No one boarded our car. The white guy at the other end looked at us without expression and then turned away. When the doors closed and we started off again, I caressed Carson's jaw, fingering his weak, sexy chin. He turned and stuck his tongue in my ear.

“Hey!”

Carson pulled his tongue away, and we both looked over at the young man on the far side of the car.

“Put your masks on!” he said loudly, not quite shouting.

He easily sat fifteen feet away, but he was, of course, completely right. And we were hardly teenagers with no place to go. “Sorry,” I said. My face felt hot.

“I don’t need you to be sorry. I need you to wear your fucking masks.”

***

My first time had been on a ferry. That is, my first time almost propositioning someone.

I was being transferred from Cagliari on the island of Sardinia to Rome and so was heading to Civitavecchia on an overnight ferry, a voyage of almost thirteen hours. It wasn’t a cruise ship. There was nothing to do. It had been raining heavily, and I’d stayed on deck as long as I could bear. The wind was cold.

But that was nicer than below deck, where everyone was crammed together. The only other respite was my “cabin,” which was hardly larger than the bunkbed itself. I suspected some passengers hadn’t been able to afford the luxury and were sleeping in their seats in the common area. I was lucky to share my room with another man, someone of course I’d never met before.

In those days, I felt like the only gay Mormon in existence, even if well aware *other* men might be gay. My bunkmate looked like a worker, though, dressed in what struck me as clothes a mechanic or bricklayer might wear, as if bricklayers wore a specific type of clothing while crossing the sea.

I was more interested in his thick, black moustache against an olive complexion and the bold, black hair on his arms.

Would it be soft? Hard like tiny wires?

I wanted to know!

I'd heard straight guys at school joking about getting blow jobs from "queers" and wondered if my bunkmate was horny enough to be interested. I was so very Mormon, unfortunately, and afraid to proposition him, not from fear he might beat me up but that it might make the Church look bad.

I took the bottom bunk, thinking that if he *did* want a blow job, he could sit on the edge of his bunk, not have to get out of bed, and I could stand and suck him off.

Assuming I knew how to do it. The terminology was confusing. Did you blow or did you suck?

With the lights out, it was quite dark. I hoped the anonymous aspect of the encounter would appeal to the guy. At least I'd had the foresight to remove my name badge when I boarded. But a young American in a white shirt and suit? Our uniform wasn't a secret.

I wanted to make a little noise fondling myself to give the guy a hint but was afraid that might scare him.

I wanted him to make a move.

I really wanted him to make a move.

I really, really, *really* wanted him to make a move.

But he just wanted to sleep.

I beat off in total silence.

***

Any trip was too long if it had to be conducted on my day off but reaching Broadway on Capitol Hill was at least relatively easy. The 106 to light rail, light rail to Capitol Hill, light rail back to Rainier Beach, and the 106 home. If I caught everything right on time, the whole trip wouldn't take more than an hour and a half, maybe two hours.

I sat one row from the doors in the last car, so I had a fighting chance of reaching the crosswalk on MLK before the No Walk sign came up and I had to wait another four minutes to head for the bus stop.

An elderly white woman with pink hair chatted with an elderly white man sporting purple hair. Tourists. Masked.

A young white woman wearing a Yale U sweatshirt boarded, her mask below her nose.

It was like owning a bike but always taking the car instead.

I tapped the Scrabble box inside my cloth bag absentmindedly. I'd gone to Lifelong specifically to get rid of a few of Brigham's things I no longer needed. I wouldn't be using his blender. I'd never wear his pants, an inch shorter than mine. And I didn't want to see his ceramic cocker spaniel any longer, the dream dog we'd never rescued.

That was more than enough to lug all the way to Capitol Hill. But it seemed dumb to make the trip and not at least peek at what new treasures I might find. I grabbed the first season of *Pushing Daisies*, a lovely purple coffee mug without any writing—I hated mugs with stupid sayings—and the Scrabble game.

At Westlake, a young white couple, both drunk, boarded with their suitcases, talking loudly about how happy they were to go back to New York. The woman was masked, but the man with her wasn't.

Did that constitute an interfaith marriage?

I'd seen a photo online of crowds along the Gulf coast in Alabama, walking maskless into a gift shop on the beach, its entrance shaped like the jaws of a shark.

An ethics professor at an Alabama university had just resigned in protest over his school's failure to require students to either mask or be vaccinated. A famous singer had announced that the vaccine had swollen her cousin's friend's testicles. A man speaking at an event with the governor of Florida claimed the vaccine changed people's RNA.

Can you spell C-R-A-Z-Y, I thought? Or B-O-N-K-E-R-S? If the K was on a double letter score…

Carson and I had played for the first time just the other night. Brigham had never cared for the word game, so I was a bit out of practice. But Carson and I listened to Bruno Mars and tried to improve on one another's performance. For instance, when Carson had made the word "raze" vertically, I'd used his "z" horizontally to write "zen." He then added a "bra" to the front of it.

When I was forced to make the pitiful word "on," Carson had added an "i" to the front of it. Inspired, I added a "pr" to the front of that. He changed my "vat" to "cravat." I changed his "just" to "adjust."

Fun.

As the tracks rose after SODO and we turned the corner to head for Beacon Hill, I noticed three dozen children's bicycles in a heap near the homeless encampment on top of the railroad tracks. A man and a woman sat on a car seat propped against a corrugated wall, kissing.

"We could fill the whole board if we had enough letters," Carson had joked.

So I'd decided to give him an extra set of tiles. I wasn't sure he'd go for it. Who wanted two z's, after all, or two q's and two x's?

But it was sure fun thinking of ways to please someone else again. I was already trying to come up with a new quilt design incorporating that last activity we'd tried from his wish list.

Too bad the nearest fabric store was in West Seattle.

***

"Nice earring." I pointed to the surgical mask hanging from the black woman's left ear.

"What?"

"Please put your mask on." I meant to say it politely, but I couldn't keep the sigh out of my voice.

And that, apparently, was enough to trigger her. She planted herself in the aisle beside me and shouted, louder than ten Tommys making inappropriate comments in public. "You're a fucking *racist*!"

I couldn't remember if I'd turned my badge around, if others could see my name and the name of my employer. If anyone was filming, this could be the day I finally got fired. "If I weren't racist," I asked carefully, "would your earring be more effective at stopping COVID?"

The woman stomped past and sat in the row directly behind me, breathing heavily, loudly, purposefully, for the next five minutes.

Lose/lose.

***

Earbud day.

The train's AC was working well in the slightly cooler weather, and it was easy to zone out of the long commute. I sat in the seat between the doors closest to the narrow hallway connecting the two halves of the car, so I had no window in the wall beside me. Which meant no late afternoon sun trying to sneak a last bit of discomfort my way.

Pink's "Raise Your Glass!" made me want to raise my glass.

Alicia Keys singing "Girl on Fire" sent so many electrical impulses across my synapses that I could barely keep from throwing my arms in the air like Maria von Trapp in the Austrian Alps.

Sia's "Cheap Thrills" felt tacky in comparison but still made me want to dance.

Green Day sang every one of their songs too loudly, but "Holiday" was pure delight. "Hey!"

I bopped my head along, barely noticing the group of four young Asian women who came up from behind and ran past me. Then an Indian woman ran by, and a young white man. It almost looked like a scene from the "Back to School" PSA put out by Sandy Hook Promise.

And then I saw a fountain of red exploding out of the young man's back like a coronal mass ejection before he went down.

I yanked out my earbuds and heard the world ending.

Chapter Twenty-Seven: Lost

Someone managed to push the red button underneath the seat in the disability section, but when the conductor heard the screams, there was little she could do. We'd just entered the Beacon Hill tunnel.

The train picked up speed, throwing the gunman off balance momentarily, but he quickly regained his footing and aimed his gun at a woman who already appeared dead. He fired.

The shooter passed me on his way into the car, chasing the more visible targets and picking them all off as they beat at the doors or tried to duck behind seats that couldn't possibly conceal them.

Images from *Stonewall* and *Schindler's List* and *Hotel Rwanda* flashed through my brain.

I debated running back through the hallway into the other half of the car, but I could see the head and arm of a man lying in the narrow passageway and didn't know how many bodies just beyond him might slow me down. Lucy Ricardo with my foot encased in cement.

"Fred, give me a hand with my foot."

All this mental calculation took less than a second. I was just about to jump up and take my chances when the gunman turned and saw me. He was too far away to hit with my bag. I pulled out my water bottle and flung it like a grenade.

"At least I'll see Brigham again," I thought.

And then I remembered Brigham wasn't waiting for me.

Sixty years, and I'd done almost nothing to make the world better. Just like the day of the police confrontation on the bus, my life didn't flash before my eyes. I didn't think of all the great friendships and lovers I'd had.

Didn't have time to wonder if their absence now was because I'd never fully given myself to them.

I thought about how giddy my death would make right-wing nutcases.

And members of my own family who'd voted against my rights every chance they had.

We reached Beacon Hill and the train lurched to a halt, knocking the shooter off balance for another moment. The doors opened, a frantic announcement began blaring, and the man aimed again.

Oh, well.

Perhaps life wasn't worth missing.

The man pulled the trigger. I tried to duck, but there was nowhere to go.

Chapter Twenty-Eight: Urban Roads, Take Me Home

"Thanks for picking me up," I said.

Carson harrumphed. "That's like thanking the sun for rising." He pinched my left nipple a little harder than necessary. "I may not be the most responsible person in the world, and I know I'm not the nicest, but come on."

"Thank you for picking me up," I repeated.

He closed his eyes and breathed out heavily. "You're welcome."

We stood on the sidewalk in front of the hospital and waited for our ride. Carson was hardly going to take me home by bus. My injuries hadn't been that bad—a graze to the head giving me a concussion and a bullet through my shoulder that had left surprisingly minimal damage—but I'd still been kept in the hospital for two nights.

Nine other passengers had died on the train. Several others, despite wounds far worse than mine, had survived. The shooter was white with no known ties to white supremacist or militia groups. The current media assessment was "the man was mentally ill."

I'd texted Carson from the hospital that first night, assuring him I was fine. "But pray for me," I typed, though he wasn't a believer, either.

Autocorrect told Carson I wanted him to "spray for me."

"Guess you can't be hurt too bad," he'd texted back.

"You OK standing?" Carson asked as we waited in front of the hospital. He'd changed his musky cologne for a musky perfume because I'd said the alcohol in colognes reminded me too much of hand sanitizer.

"Are you offering your lap?" I countered.

He shrugged. "I could throw you over my knee."

"Hmm."

Across the street, I saw a tent in front of a boarded up business. Two doors further down, a white man sat huddled with his sleeping bag around him.

"You haven't told me what you want to do this afternoon," Carson reminded me. I was to spend the whole day at his place and then stay overnight.

"We're playing Scrabble while listening to Josh Groban," I informed him.

Carson groaned. "Do I have to let you win again?"

The Logger pulled up a moment later, and Carson opened the door for me. After we settled in the back seat, the driver caught my eye in the rearview mirror. "Hi, Todd," he said. "You look like shit."

Carson turned to the driver and then to me. "Uh…"

"Carson," I said, "meet Anthony. Anthony, meet my wonderful, sweet, hot, sexy boyfriend Carson."

"OK, OK." Anthony waved over his shoulder. "I missed my shot. Congratulations, guys." His voice, I was pleased to hear, had a smile in it.

***

The shooting had seemed monumental, and yet within days, life returned to an all-too unacceptable normal. I couldn't even milk much sympathy from coworkers. Just a couple of days later, three people were killed at a bar in Burien. Yesterday, someone had boarded a school bus down in Pasco and stabbed the driver to death in front of all the kids.

Through the train window on my way home from the supermarket, I watched police officers arrest a black man on the Mount Baker station platform.

Yep, the same old normal.

And way too much of it.

My friend Jeremy in Surrey sent a link this morning to a story about a BC man who'd urinated on the counter of a fast food joint when asked to mask. During my lunch break, I watched news that anti-vaxxers in North Carolina had invaded a COVID testing site and stopped workers from conducting tests.

Alitalia declared bankruptcy and announced their last flight would be in October.

I emailed Kevin to commiserate.

But somehow, the most upsetting incident of the day had occurred just moments earlier. A short white man in a kilt, with a nose ring and at least 12 mm ear plugs, rolled his eyes when I noticed him. He stood up and moved three rows farther away as if afraid I was fantasizing about him.

Because sex with me would be a thought too repulsive to contemplate.

Goddamned irritating.

***

At the transit center, a young black teen in a hoodie and navy blue face mask stood beside the bus schedules, resting a bicycle against the railing. I wasn't sure if the slender teen was a boy or a girl. The hood, though, made me worry it was a boy. No one else was out here today. Even the mentally ill man who shouted at the ATM was gone.

"You need the 8?" the teen called out. A young man. "It's coming in two minutes."

I wanted the 48 today but didn't ask when it was arriving. The teen passed on the 8 as well when it arrived, which again worried me.

The 48 pulled up five minutes later, and since I was standing in "the spot," I almost started up the steps the moment the doors opened. But the young man seemed anxious, so I waved him ahead.

When he tried to drag his bicycle on board the bus, the driver began yelling. A newbie, I realized. I set my bag on the pavement, walked over to the front of the bus, and pulled down the bike rack. The boy joined me a second later, and I helped him set the bike in properly, showing him how to adjust the spring holder to keep it in place.

"Thanks," he said.

I nodded and waved him back aboard the bus.

***

On Staten Island, a mob of unmasked anti-vaxxers stormed the food court at a mall to protest a vaccine mandate. Anti-vaxxers had also begun inhaling hydrogen peroxide from their nebulizers.

Three people were killed and fifty more injured when Amtrak's Empire Builder derailed in Montana en route to Seattle.

There'd been more oil spills, the latest in Trinidad and Sri Lanka and Cyprus.

***

I made my way past the disability section and was scouting out empty seats near the back door when I spotted Tommy sitting on the very last row of the bus. I nodded a greeting, which he barely acknowledged, and as I continued toward him, I noticed his black eye.

I braced myself with one hand against the rear wall of the jostling bus and leaned down to kiss his forehead through my mask.

Then I sat in the corner two seats away and motioned.

Without a word, Tommy lay down, resting his head in my lap. I placed my hand on his hip and held him.

***

"No world peace—no peace in any part—without a stable climate."

Activists and advocates were marching in Australia and Belgium. They were protesting tar sands in Canada and fracking in the U.S. Reporters, though, were covering the latest mean thing one politician said about another.

Today would be my last day taking the 8 to work.

Gail's nonsense at the store had become unbearable. People across the country were quitting their jobs, no longer willing to put up with crap they'd accepted before the pandemic.

I wrote a letter to the editor of the *Seattle Times*, suggesting that people also leave crappy political parties that only gave lip service to our needs.

Equity wasn't free, and no one was offering it out of the goodness of their hearts.

I'd been accepted for a position as office support with a climate lobby. I knew most of these charities and NGOs didn't accomplish much, often developed a corporate attitude themselves, but I needed to do something that at least sometimes *felt* meaningful.

Or might on occasion help me become aware of new efforts at misdirection.

I'd put off watching *Planet of the Humans* for two years, not wanting to believe the truth about its dire assessment of our situation. Like the mass burning of forests to justify "renewable" and "net zero" policies. The film hadn't been as demoralizing as I'd expected, and I wasn't entirely sure it was 100% accurate. But things were definitely not good.

A heavy black girl, maybe twelve, boarded wearing an overstuffed backpack.

A white woman carrying a cup of coffee sat across the aisle from her. The first thing she did after setting her bag on the seat was pull down her mask to sip her coffee.

Perhaps natural selection had already selected us for extinction.

Last night, an official from the former administration warned people that the CDC was putting COVID vaccines in salad dressing.

Right-wing school boards were firing teachers they accused of teaching Critical Race Theory. More books were being banned, the latest *Hidden Figures* and *The Absolutely True Diary of a Part-Time Indian.* School boards in two states wanted to present "both sides" when presenting lessons about the Holocaust.

Texas had just passed a law allowing anyone, from any state, to sue any person involved in any way with helping a woman seek a legal abortion, even if the litigant had no connection to the pregnant woman or any other person involved.

People could sue a relative who loaned their niece money or a Lyft driver who transported the woman to a clinic. In theory, they could even sue the driver of a bus the woman had taken to get to the clinic on her own. The bounty for suing complete strangers was $10,000.

"Welcome to Gilead" memes were everywhere.

Two lawsuits had already been filed against a doctor.

A politician in Texas was advocating for "Texit," suggesting a right-wing radio host be made their president. A group in Idaho was openly advocating for theocracy.

The white woman a few rows ahead of me apparently sipped her coffee the wrong way and started choking. She coughed for at least a minute, occasionally covering her mouth with her elbow.

But never her mask.

My phone pinged, and I saw a text from Carson. "Today is the first day of the rest of your life."

I smiled and texted back. "No, it's the 43rd day. The first day was when I met you."

***

"All douched out and nowhere to go." I put my hands on my hips. "You told me to be ready."

We stood on the platform at Stadium station after Carson clocked out at work. And now he was asking me to go north to the U District rather than to his place.

"I want you to meet Navid," he said.

I frowned, though Carson couldn't see under my mask. "Are we having a three-way?" I asked. We certainly weren't heading to dinner at this hour.

"No three-way."

I wasn't sure if I was disappointed or not. So many people were behaving in sexually reckless ways after being cooped up for a year and a half. With death in the news every day, I understood.

It had felt morbidly appropriate a few days earlier to visit the Conservatory in Volunteer Park and witness the corpse flower's huge Audrey II tongue and smell its nauseating fragrance. The flower bloomed unpredictably, every seven to ten years or so. When Carson heard the news, he texted me and I headed over immediately after work. The greenhouse was closed by the time he finished his shift, so he hadn't been able to join me.

A rumble to the south grew louder as the train approached. When it stopped in front of us, we climbed aboard and found seats in the last row.

"Navid is a friend of mine," Carson explained. "He works in an STD clinic up by the university."

Merde. I hadn't thought about Richard in a long time. "So…?"

"I remembered what you said," Carson continued. "When I told Navid about it, he said *he'd* been fantasizing about a sex party at work after hours."

"Oh. My. God."

Carson squeezed my thigh. "Navid's about to retire, so it's pretty much now or never."

Eat, drink, and be merry, for tomorrow...

"He's invited us and five other guys." Carson now tweaked my right nipple. "Plus his partner. It's safer sex only."

A quick calculation showed we'd be a little short of my fantasy total.

Where were the Three Nephites when you needed them?

"I asked if I could film tonight's activities."

I felt a rush of adrenalin.

"We can't post it, obviously, but I thought it'd be something we could watch together once in a while." He nudged his shoulder against mine. "With or without company."

I thought about the SNL "It Gets Better" sketch.

"You know what your best quality is?" I said, resting my head on his shoulder.

“Todd,” Carson warned me, “we only have fifteen minutes before we get to the UW station.”

“You remember even the stupid things I say.”

“Oh, honey,” he said, kissing the top of my head. “What else is it you think you say?”

Chapter Twenty-Nine: A Journey Makes Itself Necessary

"I like your shirt," Carson said.

"I like the man who gave it to me," I replied.

"Like?"

"Lust after?" I tried clarifying. "Feel warmly toward? Admire?"

"'*Admire*'? Fuck that!"

"OK. It's about time you became more versatile."

"I'm plenty versatile!" he said. "Think of all the positions we've already tried. Especially when we had that three-way with Samuel." A young white man, perhaps thirty, glanced in our direction. I chose to interpret his expression as jealousy. He was quickly distracted, though, when a black man his age wearing tight jeans boarded a moment later.

I fingered my new T-shirt. "'You have to be kind to be kind.'" Not as catchy as Nick Lowe's version but more accurate.

Advertising I could live with.

Carson and I were heading downtown for a protest in front of City Hall. Demonstrations of one sort or another popped up across Seattle every few weeks. No one even paid attention anymore other than to bitch about traffic being rerouted. Despite assertions about the importance of addressing climate change, actual policies here and pretty much everywhere else fell far short of what was required. Many local governments and universities still refused even to divest from fossil fuels.

Greta Thunberg blasted world leaders at the Youth4Climate conference in Milano with her eloquent "blah blah blah" speech.

One researcher predicted that between three and five billion people would die in the coming decade from food and water shortages.

My sign read "Is capitalism more sacred than a livable climate?" I'd covered the posterboard with clear plastic to protect it in case of rain.

Carson's was easier to grasp. "What have you got against a stable climate?"

Three young black women, wearing eye shadow to match their hijabs, boarded the bus on MLK. They carried signs, too. "System change, not climate change."

"Instead of terraforming Mars, let's keep Earth habitable."

"You think the immigration crisis is bad now, just wait till there's even more CO_2 in the atmosphere!"

I shook my head. It was too long. News clips grew shorter and shorter, attention spans shrinking as the time left to watch them evaporated.

"Thanks, honey," Carson said, leaning over to kiss me.

"For what?"

"Making me feel alive."

I knew Carson had spent almost $20 on my shirt, and as much as I loved the gift, I had to wonder about all the ways we contributed to the climate crisis ourselves.

Was there really any point in buying a DVD of *Last Holiday*, even if I loved Queen Latifah?

Last night, I'd seen a news report about anti-masker members of a white supremacist group infiltrating two schools in the southern part of the state near Vancouver. Border agents in Texas were using whips against some of the 10,000 undocumented immigrants, mostly Haitians relocating after an earthquake devastated their island, huddling under a bridge along the Rio Grande.

Two Asian teens, a young man and a young woman, boarded the bus carrying signs. One stop later, a white couple in their thirties boarded with a five-year-old. All three were carrying signs. The young girl's read, "I want to grow up."

***

I waved to the young white man wearing a Huskies sweatshirt and pointed. He frowned back at me. I pointed again.

"What?" he said. Carson sat beside me on the train in silence. It was late, and there were perhaps five other people in our car.

"You have something on your nose," I explained.

The man rubbed the tip of his nose and then looked at his fingers. He glared in my direction.

"I'm sorry," I said. "What I *meant* to say is that you *don't* have something on your nose." I pointed to his lower face. "Why don't you pull that mask up a little higher?"

In Italy, talking to people on the street had been pure agony. Knocking on doors had been only slightly more bearable because my companion and I used to sit on the top landing in each building and chat for a few minutes to ease the pain.

One time, residents came out with guns and chased us from the building.

"Shut up, man. It keeps slipping."

The passengers nearest us on the light rail were pretending the conversation wasn't taking place, but those farther away were watching cautiously. This time of evening, folks were either heading home or to the airport. We all just wanted a little peace. But shutting up wasn't exactly the same thing.

Carson pulled out his phone and started filming.

"Sure," I said. "I get it. But you have a job, right?"

The man continued glaring.

"If you went to work with pants that kept slipping below your dick, and you weren't wearing underwear, do you think HR would say something?"

Now the passengers closest to us were watching, too.

"Would your boss or coworkers look at your dick twenty times a day and accept 'My pants keep slipping' as reasonable?"

I stepped into the aisle and unzipped but didn't reach past my turquoise boxer briefs. Carson continued filming.

"Fuck you, man."

"No." I shook my head. "Let's try something different."

The man frowned and hunched forward slightly, his muscles tensed. I didn't know how anyone else was reacting, afraid to break eye contact. I hoped the guy would just decide that refusing to properly mask wasn't worth the trouble.

But what I really wondered was if calling people out for it was.

"Let's do an HIV test," I said. "I'll fuck you while wearing a condom on my finger and he'll fuck you with one on his dick." I nodded toward Carson. "Then we'll see which method is more effective at preventing infection."

There were no known cases of men with undetectable viral loads passing the virus on to anyone, so it was a moot point, but the man jumped up and ran to the door at the far end of the car as we entered the Beacon Hill station, banging on the glass to will the driver to open immediately. Just before he stepped out, I called after the guy one last time. "Pull up your pants!"

I zipped mine back up.

We were all hypocrites sometimes, but Jesus H. Christ in a sling.

"You really can be an asshole," Carson said as the doors closed and we began heading south again. None of the other passengers had moved. Seasoned commuters, I supposed.

"And a dick," I admitted. "A versatile jerk."

"I guess that's why I love you."

The first time either of us had used the word.

Without warning, Carson dropped to one knee in the middle of the aisle, still filming while awkwardly reaching into his left pocket and extracting a silver ring in a tiny plastic bag. "I wasn't going to propose so soon," he said, "but we want the event to be unforgettable, don't we?"

I swallowed and gasped at the same time, choking on my spit, and remembering the SNL skit making fun of Natalie Cole's song.

It was way too early to move in together. And way too late to waste time.

"The answer is yes," I said, coughing another few moments, "to both questions." When I was sure the choking fit was over, I leaned down to kiss him, still masked, surprised to hear the other passengers in the car cheering.

***

The Nisqually Tribe had sequestered several cabins on their tribal land so that Natives who'd tested positive for COVID could self-quarantine and avoid infecting family members. But some paranoid right-wing conspiracy nut had "discovered" the place and decided the government was setting up concentration camps for unvaccinated Americans. He posted the location online and urged fellow patriots to come "do something about this."

The folks quarantining fled to a hotel to wait out their infection.

***

"Why don't you come by our place this weekend?" the man said. Daniel was white, his partner Cliff Eurasian, both in their late thirties. When they boarded the 11 a few minutes earlier, they sat in the row directly in front of me. I was down to 210 pounds but still nowhere near a societally acceptable weight. I pedaled on my stationary bike now simply because it made me feel good.

"We have HEPA air filters," Cliff coaxed.

"Bring your fiancé," Daniel added. They'd wasted no time in getting all the essential information before making their proposal.

Cliff pulled the cord, and the two men hopped off the bus at the next stop. I checked my watch and sent Carson a quick text. At this time of day, he was probably on his lunch break.

"We're playing Scrabble with some cute guys on Saturday." I included a photo of the two men.

"Is that all we're playing?" he texted back a few moments later.

"Afraid so."

"Then why did you send a picture of them kissing?"

They'd willingly posed, their masks touching, but didn't appear interested in sharing anything more intimate. "Because I love getting you horny in the middle of your shift."

"That's shaft," he corrected, "and the whole damn thing is horny now."

***

The white woman boarding the bus couldn't have been over fifty. Her clothes were clean, though not particularly impressive, her hair dyed a mousy brown.

Really, if you were choosing your hair color…

She'd been ahead of me in the grocery store, too, and had purchased a small box of baking soda, a box of Epsom salt, and a box of sodium tetraborate. I knew the chemical makeup because the recipe for the home treatment the woman was obviously planning had been on the news the past few days.

People across the country who'd been "forced" by their employers to accept vaccination were now taking baths in these chemicals to "reverse" the immunization. Some were also making incisions at the injection site and using the medieval practice of cupping to draw the shot's "nanotechnologies" out of their bodies.

The woman sat in the disabled section, pulling her mask off as soon as she passed the driver. After I tapped my card, I reached into my shopping bag and grabbed a strawberry protein bar.

"Here, ma'am." I offered it to the woman as I passed. "You'll need your strength tonight." I nodded toward her bag.

She looked unsure if I was a confederate or an enemy.

She scowled.

I guess she'd made up her mind.

***

Homeless people were camping along the edges of Cal Anderson Park. A tent had been erected in the alley between two buildings across the street in a way to avoid obstructing the garbage collection crew.

Life in the Emerald City, home to two of the richest men in America.

We weren't peasants working the king's fields. We were drowning in his sewage-filled moat.

This wasn't a downturn. Things weren't going to get better. When Kevin and I had walked through the

Coliseum in Rome, we'd talked about what witnessing the fall of the Roman Empire must have been like. Were people even aware what was happening as it occurred?

What we were witnessing now might not even be the fall of the American Empire but the fall of human civilization. If we all pulled together, I hoped—I despaired—we might still be able to save ourselves.

"Hey!" I could hear Mickey Rooney telling Judy Garland. "Let's put on a show!"

That ship, I knew, had sailed.

That train had left the station.

The trolley, too.

Poor Judy.

The bus crossed Broadway and stopped in front of the old Egyptian Theater, all boarded up now. I pulled out my phone and texted Carson.

"I'll meet you at Stadium station when you get off work," I said, "ready to fall ever more deeply in love with you."

He texted back several minutes later. "How deeply?"

"Deeply enough to let you do that thing you've been asking about for the past two weeks."

"About time," he said, "but you should know I've used those two weeks to think about ways to make the experience much more memorable."

Did they make drugs to help people forget consensual sex?

I wanted to remember every second of my time with Carson.

The way I remembered the alien in *Starman* explaining his assessment of humans to Karen Allen. "Shall I tell you what I find beautiful about you?" I'd wanted so badly to look like Jeff Bridges.

I *did* look like him now.

"'You are at your very best when things are worst,'" I quoted into the phone.

"OMG, Todd," Carson texted back. "You've got me so worked up I'll have to ask this guy waiting for the bus to join me in the bathroom."

"Don't do anything I wouldn't do."

"Not sure that's possible."

"XO."

"FU."

***

The Washington State fair had drawn over 816,000 visitors over the past month to Puyallup. Outdoors, so reasonably safe, but in all the photos of the vast crowds milling about together for hours, I didn't see a single mask.

We all just wanted to live in the past. And with a present so awful and a future that might never exist, who could blame us?

We were Mariette Hartley in "All Our Yesterdays."

***

"When do you think this rain will end?" a woman asked her partner as we headed north through SODO. Tourists.

"April," I said from across the aisle. The white couple were both masked, so I felt generous with my knowledge. I was also excited that light rail had opened three new stations past UW this morning.

Today's drizzle had put me in a good mood, too. I was heading downtown, where I'd transfer to the 40 and then to Fremont for work. On the way home later, I'd stop at Safeway. I might even pick up some chocolate syrup for Carson.

The drought was over for now. Or at least wouldn't grow any worse until next spring.

Down in Sacramento, after 212 days straight with no rain—their longest stretch ever—they'd just received 5.44 inches in one day, their largest ever one-day total.

I pulled out my phone and texted Debryant to see how things at his new home in Calistoga were going.

***

"What's that smell?" a white woman asked a white man on the train next to her. They were both in their upper forties. She wrinkled her nose, which was plainly visible.

The man looked down at his shoe.

"Shit!" he said.

The woman finally covered her face…with her hands.

"Must have stepped on it in the elevator," the man said, his face reddening. He stood and scraped his shoe against the partition separating the seats from the open area near the doors.

"All these homeless people!" the woman said, loudly enough to be heard through her hands. "Seattle's *horrible*!"

She was right, of course.

"Should we just kill them all?" I asked.

Several people around me gasped. The woman gasped as well. "What's *wrong* with you people?" She huddled even closer to the wall beside her. When her husband moved to comfort her, she recoiled from him, too, unable to stop herself from glancing at his feet.

Tourists had to deal with human shit and piss, Seattle residents had to deal with it, and Seattle's unhoused had to deal with it.

But that was a choice. City officials *could* provide portable toilets. They simply believed that punishing the destitute miraculously put a stop to normal bodily functions.

Laws were designed to punish "inappropriate" sex, too, especially that of gay men meeting up in the bushes of this or that park, but really, the same moral failure was to blame—our need to punish those whose lives didn't fit the mold we felt they should.

If city officials didn't want to see sex in public, they could make portable sex rooms available as easily as they could furnish public toilets, as easily as they could provide clean needle exchanges, as easily as they could fill a dozen other human needs that might have prevented a hundred thousand Americans from dying of overdoses in the past twelve months.

It was simply more important for us to punish rather than solve, this self-destructive impulse the main reason those on the far right denied climate change, too. It allowed them to "own the libs."

Now, of course, people of all political ideologies, even their own, would have to deal with the consequences of petty revenge.

On the whole, humans were reasonably cooperative. There'd be no other way to build roads or airplanes, to run businesses or governments.

To establish bus routes.

But this single flaw—vindictiveness—was enough to seal our fate.

***

Heavy rains and flooding in southern Egypt drove hordes of scorpions into nearby towns. Hundreds of people had been hospitalized from the stings.

Flooding in British Columbia had washed out roads, bridges, and rail lines in every direction leaving Vancouver. The port city was now cut off from the rest of Canada. Sewage filled the streets of Merritt. A hundred RVs burned in Abbotsford, no one able to reach the flames and douse them.

Rossiglione, a town just south of Milano, was inundated with over 29 inches of rain in twelve hours, a record accumulation for anywhere on the entire European continent. Ever.

***

A middle-aged, obese white woman with a walker sat in the disabled section, talking on her phone. Her gray hair was long, unusual for a woman her age. Several stops later, when a heavyset, older black woman boarded in a wheelchair, the woman in the walker pulled up the disability bench and helped secure the incoming chair with a seatbelt so the driver didn't have to. Then she moved a couple of rows deeper into the bus and squeezed into one of the rows there.

On the news last night, I listened to parents in eastern Washington yelling at school board members. "Masks are child abuse!"

Another batch of fake vaccination cards was intercepted heading to a state full of anti-vaxxers.

Four men with zip ties tried to make a citizen's arrest of a school principal in Tucson after she sent a boy home because he'd been exposed to COVID in class.

A young Latino, masked, moved to the rear door and pressed the Stop Requested button next to it. He then removed his mask while waiting for the bus to pull over to the curb. A black woman, maybe thirty, held a mask to her face as she boarded up front, stuffing it in her pocket as soon as she moved past the driver.

COVID cases in the U.S. were falling for the third week in a row. No one really understood why. Anti-maskers and anti-vaxxers felt vindicated. Perhaps they were.

I was keeping my mask on for a while longer. And my booster was scheduled for next week.

But everything wasn't about COVID. A shame, since sooner or later, the virus, while it might never disappear, would almost certainly fade into the background.

A man dressed as the Joker had just stabbed seventeen riders on the subway in Tokyo. Video showed terrified passengers scrambling out the windows. In Northern Ireland, a man poured gasoline into a bus and set the vehicle on fire. No passengers were on board at the time, and the driver managed to escape.

I no longer remembered what it felt like to be safe. Perhaps that feeling had never been more than an illusion to begin with.

As a missionary, I'd been taught to seek converts among those who'd just experienced a major upheaval in their lives. Nearly being murdered probably counted. But I wasn't sure what I was converting to. I remembered Téa

Leoni in *Deep Impact* telling the congressman, "We know about ELE," then slowly realizing her own life was about to end.

Just like Téa, I understood I wasn't going to be one of the survivors. Too old, too fat, too much nerve damage in my feet. Even if I lost all this excess weight—and that wasn't likely—I was still no match for twenty-year-olds fighting for a chance to feed their kids.

And I didn't *want* to eat food their kids needed.

Carson, younger and in far better shape, probably wouldn't be one of the survivors, either. The best we could do was live and love, be good to each other while we could.

"Fate ciò che potete," I remembered, "con ciò che avete, dove siete."

I loved that Carson wanted to watch *Luisa Spagnoli* with me.

Too bad we'd never be able to travel to Italy together.

And a shame there was no eternal reward awaiting us no matter our behavior, no one to remember that for a fleeting moment in time we mattered to someone.

I'd be meeting him tonight at Stadium station, we'd study our third ASL lesson back at his place, and then we'd make love in the dark, listening to the rain pattering softly against the windows.

***

Earbud day.

ABBA's "Knowing Me, Knowing You" was sad but sweet.

Their "Gimme! Gimme! Gimme! A Man after Midnight" put a smile on my face, thinking of tonight's date with Carson.

"Does Your Mother Know?" was pure fun, and a reminder that the male members of ABBA could sing quite well, too.

"Take a Chance on Me." If there was one thing I knew, it was that reality rarely rated above a 6 or a 7. We were lucky to get a 5, no matter what Toni Colette said.

But when ABBA's first new song in forty years began playing, "I Still Have Faith in You," I knew things were somehow, despite everything, going to be all right.

Or at least as all right as they needed to be.

About the Author

Johnny Townsend earned an MFA in fiction writing from Louisiana State University. He was also awarded a BA and MA in English, as well as a BS in Biology. A native of New Orleans, Townsend relocated to Seattle in the aftermath of Hurricane Katrina.

After attending a Baptist high school for four years as a teenager, he volunteered as a Mormon missionary in Italy and then held positions in his local New Orleans ward as Second Councilor in the Elders Quorum, Ward Single Adult Representative, Stake Single Adult Chair, Sunday School Teacher, Stake Missionary, and Ward Membership Clerk.

In the secular world, Townsend worked as a bookstore clerk, college English instructor, bank teller, loan processor, mail carrier, library associate, receptionist, and professional escort. He worked selling bus passes, installing insulation, delivering pizza, cleaning residential construction sites, rehabilitating developmentally disabled adults, surveying gas stations, translating documents from Italian into English, selling porn and dildos, preparing surgical carts for medical teams, and performing experiments on rat brains in a physiology lab.

Townsend has published stories and essays in *Newsday, The Washington Post, The Los Angeles Times, The Salt Lake Tribune, The Seattle Times, The Orlando Sentinel, The Army Times, The Humanist, The Progressive, Bay Area Reporter, Medical Reform, Christopher Street, The Massachusetts Review, Glimmer Train, Sunstone, Dialogue: A Journal of Mormon Thought*, in the anthologies *Queer Fish, Off the Rocks, Moth and Rust, The Kindness of Strangers,* and *In Our Lovely Deseret: Mormon Fictions.* He helped edit *Latter-Gay Saints*, a collection of stories about gay Mormons, and he is the author of 52 books.

Most of those books are collections of Mormon short stories, several of which were named to Kirkus Reviews' Best of the Year lists. In addition to his Mormon stories, Townsend has written several M/M romances and a collection of Jewish stories, *The Golem of Rabbi Loew.*

He has also written one non-fiction book, *Let the Faggots Burn: The UpStairs Lounge Fire*, after interviewing survivors as well as friends and relatives of the 32 people who were killed when an arsonist set fire to a gay bar in the French Quarter of New Orleans on Gay Pride Day in 1973. He is an Associate Producer of the feature-length documentary *Upstairs Inferno*, directed by Robert Camina.

Johnny Townsend is married to Gary Tolman, another former Mormon who worked in the same mission in Italy. They still speak Italian to each other regularly.

Books by Johnny Townsend

Thanks for reading! If you enjoyed this book, could you please take a few minutes to write a review online? Reviews are helpful both to me as an author and to other readers, so we'd all sincerely appreciate your writing one! And if you did enjoy the book, here are some others I've written you might want to look up:

Mormon Underwear

The Circumcision of God

Sex among the Saints

Zombies for Jesus

The Abominable Gayman

The Gay Mormon Quilter's Club

The Golem of Rabbi Loew

Flying over Babel

Marginal Mormons

The Mormon Victorian Society

Dragons of the Book of Mormon

Selling the City of Enoch

Gayrabian Nights

Lying for the Lord

Missionaries Make the Best Companions

Invasion of the Spirit Snatchers

The Tyranny of Silence

Sex on the Sabbath

The Washing of Brains

The Mormon Inquisition

The Moat around Zion

The Last Days Linger

Mormon Madness

Human Compassion for Beginners

Dead Mankind Walking

Breaking the Promise of the Promised Land

Am I My Planet's Keeper?

Have Your Cum and Eat It, Too

Strangers with Benefits

What Would Anne Frank Do?

Wake Up and Smell the Missionaries

Quilting Beyond the Rainbow

Gay Sleeping Arrangements

Queer Quilting

Racism by Proxy

Orgy at the STD Clinic

Let the Faggots Burn: The UpStairs Lounge Fire

Latter-Gay Saints: An Anthology of Gay Mormon Fiction (co-editor)

Available from BookLocker.com or your favorite online or neighborhood bookstore.

Wondering what some of those other books are about? Read on!

Invasion of the Spirit Snatchers

During the Apocalypse, a group of Mormon survivors in Hurricane, Utah gather in the home of the Relief Society president, telling stories to pass the time as they ration their food storage and await the Second Coming. But this is no ordinary group of Mormons—or perhaps it is. They are the faithful, feminist, gay, apostate, and repentant, all working together to help each other through the darkest days any of them have yet seen.

Gayrabian Nights

Gayrabian Nights is a twist on the well-known classic, *1001 Arabian Nights*, in which Scheherazade, under the threat of death if she ceases to captivate King Shahryar's attention, enchants him through a series of mysterious, adventurous, and romantic tales.

In this variation, a male escort, invited to the hotel room of a closeted, homophobic Mormon senator, learns that the man is poised to vote on a piece of anti-gay legislation the following morning. To prevent him from sleeping, so that the exhausted senator will miss casting his vote on the Senate floor, the escort entertains him with stories of homophobia, celibacy, mixed orientation marriages, reparative therapy, coming out, first love, gay marriage, and long-term successful gay relationships. The escort crafts the stories to give the senator a crash course in gay culture and sensibilities, hoping to bring the man closer to accepting his own sexual orientation.

Let the Faggots Burn: The UpStairs Lounge Fire

On Gay Pride Day in 1973, someone set the entrance to a French Quarter gay bar on fire. In the terrible inferno that followed, thirty-two people lost their lives, including a third of the local congregation of the Metropolitan Community Church, their pastor burning to death halfway out a second-story window as he tried to claw his way to freedom. A mother who'd gone to the bar with her two gay sons died alongside them. A man who'd helped his friend escape first was found dead near the fire escape. Two children waited outside a movie theater across town for a father and step-father who would never pick them up. During this era of rampant homophobia, several families refused to claim the bodies, and many churches refused to bury the dead. Author Johnny Townsend pored through old records and tracked down survivors of the fire as well as relatives and friends of those killed to compile this fascinating account of a forgotten moment in gay history.

Am I My Planet's Keeper?

Global Warming. Climate Change. Climate Crisis. Climate Emergency. Whatever label we use, we are facing one of the greatest challenges to the survival of life as we know it.

But while addressing greenhouse gases is perhaps our most urgent need, it's not our only task. We must also address toxic waste, pollution, habitat destruction, and our other contributions to the world's sixth mass extinction event.

In order to do that, we must simultaneously address the unmet human needs that keep us distracted from deeper engagement in stabilizing our climate: moderating economic inequality, guaranteeing healthcare to all, and ensuring education for everyone.

And to accomplish *that*, we must unite to combat the monied forces that use fear, prejudice, and misinformation to manipulate us.

It's a daunting task. But success is our only option.

Wake Up and Smell the Missionaries

Two Mormon missionaries in Italy discover they share the same rare ability—both can emit pheromones on demand. At first, they playfully compete in the hills of Frascati to see who can tempt "investigators" most. But soon they're targeting each other non-stop.

Can two immature young men learn to control their "superpower" to live a normal life…and develop genuine love? Even as their relationship is threatened by the attentions of another man?

They seem just on the verge of success when a massive earthquake leaves them trapped under the rubble of their apartment in Castellammare.

With night falling and temperatures dropping, can they dig themselves out in time to save themselves? And will their injuries destroy the ability that brought them together in the first place?

What Readers Have Said

Townsend's stories are "a gay *Portnoy's Complaint* of Mormonism. Salacious, sweet, sad, insightful, insulting, religiously ethnic, quirky-faithful, and funny."

D. Michael Quinn, author of *The Mormon Hierarchy: Origins of Power*

"Told from a believably conversational first-person perspective, [*The Abominable Gayman*'s] novelistic focus on Anderson's journey to thoughtful self-acceptance allows for greater character development than often seen in short stories, which makes this well-paced work rich and satisfying, and one of Townsend's strongest. An extremely important contribution to the field of Mormon fiction." Named to Kirkus Reviews' Best of 2011.

Kirkus Reviews

"The thirteen stories in *Mormon Underwear* capture this struggle [between Mormonism and homosexuality] with humor, sadness, insight, and sometimes shocking details....*Mormon Underwear* provides compelling stories, literally from the inside-out."

Niki D'Andrea, *Phoenix New Times*

"Townsend's lively writing style and engaging characters [in *Zombies for Jesus*] make for stories which force us to wake up, smell the (prohibited) coffee, and review our attitudes with regard to reading dogma so doggedly. These are tales which revel in the individual tics and quirks which make us human, Mormon or not, gay or not..."

A.J. Kirby, *The Short Review*

"The Rift," from *The Abominable Gayman*, is a "fascinating tale of an untenable situation...a *tour de force*."

David Lenson, editor, *The Massachusetts Review*

"Pronouncing the Apostrophe," from *The Golem of Rabbi Loew*, is "quiet and revealing, an intriguing tale..."

Sima Rabinowitz, Literary Magazine Review, *NewPages.com*

The Circumcision of God is "a collection of short stories that consider the imperfect, silenced majority of Mormons, who may in fact be [the Church's] best hope....[The book leaves] readers regretting the church's willingness to marginalize those who best exemplify its ideals: those who love fiercely despite all obstacles, who brave challenges at great personal risk and who always choose the hard, higher road."

Kirkus Reviews

In *Mormon Fairy Tales*, Johnny Townsend displays "both a wicked sense of irony and a deep well of compassion."

Kel Munger, *Sacramento News and Review*

Zombies for Jesus is "eerie, erotic, and magical."

Publishers Weekly

"While [Townsend's] many touching vignettes draw deeply from Mormon mythology, history, spirituality and culture, [*Mormon Fairy Tales*] is neither a gaudy act of proselytism nor angry protest literature from an ex-believer. Like all good fiction, his stories are simply about the joys, the hopes and the sorrows of people."

Kirkus Reviews

"In *Let the Faggots Burn* author Johnny Townsend restores this tragic event [the UpStairs Lounge fire] to its proper place in LGBT history and reminds us that the victims of the blaze were not just 'statistics,' but real people with real lives, families, and friends."

Jesse Monteagudo, *The Bilerico Project*

In *Let the Faggots Burn*, "Townsend's heart-rending descriptions of the victims…seem to [make them] come alive once more."

Kit Van Cleave, *OutSmart Magazine*

Marginal Mormons is "an irreverent, honest look at life outside the mainstream Mormon Church….Throughout his musings on sin and forgiveness, Townsend beautifully demonstrates his characters' internal, perhaps irreconcilable struggles….Rather than anger and disdain, he offers an honest portrayal of people searching for meaning and community in their lives, regardless of their life choices or secrets." Named to Kirkus Reviews' Best of 2012.

Kirkus Reviews

The stories in *The Mormon Victorian Society* "register the new openness and confidence of gay life in the age of same-sex marriage….What hasn't changed is Townsend's wry, conversational prose, his subtle evocations of character and social dynamics, and his deadpan humor. His warm empathy still glows in this intimate yet clear-eyed engagement with Mormon theology and folkways. Funny, shrewd and finely wrought dissections of the awkward contradictions—and surprising harmonies—between conscience and desire." Named to Kirkus Reviews' Best of 2013.

Kirkus Reviews

"This collection of short stories [*The Mormon Victorian Society*] featuring gay Mormon characters slammed [me] in the face from the first page, wrestled my heart and mind to the floor, and left me panting and wanting more by the end. Johnny Townsend has created so many memorable characters in such few pages. I went weeks thinking about this book. It truly touched me."

Tom Webb, *A Bear on Books*

Dragons of the Book of Mormon is an "entertaining collection....Townsend's prose is sharp, clear, and easy to read, and his characters are well rendered..."

Publishers Weekly

"The pre-eminent documenter of alternative Mormon lifestyles...Townsend has a deep understanding of his characters, and his limpid prose, dry humor and well-grounded (occasionally magical) realism make their spiritual conundrums both compelling and entertaining. [*Dragons of the Book of Mormon* is] [a]nother of Townsend's critical but affectionate and absorbing tours of Mormon discontent." Named to Kirkus Reviews' Best of 2014.

Kirkus Reviews

In *Gayrabian Nights*, "Townsend's prose is always limpid and evocative, and…he finds real drama and emotional depth in the most ordinary of lives."

Kirkus Reviews

Gayrabian Nights is a "complex revelation of how seriously soul damaging the denial of the true self can be."

Ryan Rhodes, author of *Free Electricity*

Gayrabian Nights "was easily the most original book I've read all year. Funny, touching, topical, and thoroughly enjoyable."

Rainbow Awards

Lying for the Lord is "one of the most gripping books that I've picked up for quite a while. I love the author's writing style, alternately cynical, humorous, biting, scathing, poignant, and touching…. This is the third book of his that I've read, and all are equally engaging. These are stories that need to be told, and the author does it in just the right way."

Heidi Alsop, *Ex-Mormon Foundation Board Member*

In *Lying for the Lord*, Townsend "gets under the skin of his characters to reveal their complexity and conflicts....shrewd, evocative [and] wryly humorous."

Kirkus Reviews

In *Missionaries Make the Best Companions*, "the author treats the clash between religious dogma and liberal humanism with vivid realism, sly humor, and subtle feeling as his characters try to figure out their true missions in life. Another of Townsend's rich dissections of Mormon failures and uncertainties..." Named to Kirkus Reviews' Best of 2015.

Kirkus Reviews

In *Invasion of the Spirit Snatchers*, "Townsend, a confident and practiced storyteller, skewers the hypocrisies and eccentricities of his characters with precision and affection. The outlandish framing narrative is the most consistent source of shock and humor, but the stories do much to ground the reader in the world—or former world—of the characters....A funny, charming tale about a group of Mormons facing the end of the world."

Kirkus Reviews

"Townsend's collection [*The Washing of Brains*] once again displays his limpid, naturalistic prose, skillful narrative chops, and his subtle insights into psychology…Well-crafted dispatches on the clash between religion and self-fulfillment…"

Kirkus Reviews

"While the author is generally at his best when working as a satirist, there are some fine, understated touches in these tales [*The Last Days Linger*] that will likely affect readers in subtle ways….readers should come away impressed by the deep empathy he shows for all his characters—even the homophobic ones."

Kirkus Reviews

"Written in a conversational style that often uses stories and personal anecdotes to reveal larger truths, this immensely approachable book [*Racism by Proxy*] skillfully serves its intended audience of White readers grappling with complex questions regarding race, history, and identity. The author's frequent references to the Church of Jesus Christ of Latter-day Saints may be too niche for readers unfamiliar with its idiosyncrasies, but Townsend generally strikes a perfect balance of humor, introspection, and reasoned arguments that will engage even skeptical readers."

Kirkus Reviews

CPSIA information can be obtained
at www.ICGtesting.com
Printed in the USA
BVHW072355090322
630953BV00001BA/3

9 781647 199388